The
LONDON BLITZ MURDERS

MAX ALLAN COLLINS

BERKLEY PRIME CRIME, NEW YORK

THE LONDON BLITZ MURDERS

A Berkley Prime Crime Book / published by arrangement with the author

PRINTING HISTORY
Berkley Prime Crime edition / May 2004

ISBN: 0-425-19805-7

Berkley Prime Crime Books are published
by The Berkley Publishing Group,
a division of Penguin Group (USA) Inc.,
375 Hudson Street, New York, New York 10014.
The name BERKLEY PRIME CRIME and the BERKLEY PRIME CRIME design are trademarks belonging to Penguin Group (USA) Inc.

PRINTED IN THE UNITED STATES OF AMERICA

10 9 8 7 6 5 4 3 2 1

In memory of
JaNiece Mull,
who loved Agatha Christie

Praise for
The Lusitania Murders

"Entertaining . . . full of colorful characters . . . a stirring conclusion."
—Detroit Free Press

"Collins ably weaves a well-paced, closed-environment mystery reminiscent of Agatha Christie . . . [He] succeeds in . . . re-imagining the *Lusitania's* final voyage."
—Publishers Weekly

The Titanic Murders

"Collins makes it sound as though it really happened."
—New York Daily News

"Collins does a fine job of insinuating a mystery into a world-famous disaster . . . [he] manage[s] to raise plenty of goose bumps before the ship goes down for the count."
—Mystery News

The Hindenburg Murders

"Max Allan Collins has become one of the masters of the twentieth-century historical mystery and *The Hindenburg Murders* will only augment his growing reputation."
—BookBrowser

The Pearl Harbor Murders

"[Collins's] descriptions are so vivid and colorful that it's like watching a movie . . . [and he] gives the reader a front row seat."
—Cozies, Capers & Crimes

continued . . .

... and for Max Allan Collins

"Max Allan Collins blends fact and fiction like no other writer."   —Andrew Vachss, author of *Flood*

"A terrific writer!"   —Mickey Spillane

"Collins displays a compelling talent for flowing narrative and concise, believable dialogue."   —*Library Journal*

"No one fictionalizes real-life mysteries better."
—*Armchair Detective*

"An uncanny ability to blend fact and fiction."
—*South Bend Tribune*

Though this work is a work of fiction, an underpinning of history supports the events depicted in these pages. The author intends no disrespect for the real people who inspired the characterizations herein, nor to take lightly the two wartime reigns of terror they endured—the Blitz . . . and the Blackout Ripper.

"The truth is that no one never believes for a minute—no matter what danger you're in—that you yourself are going to be killed. The bomb is always going to hit the other person."

Agatha Christie

BEFORE . . .

On the brink of war, London was the largest and—in the opinion of many—greatest city in the world. Metropolitan London's population was eight million and ever-growing, the population of Great Britain herself having risen some five million souls between the First War and the coming one . . . a third of whom lived or worked in London.

The Port of London commanded more tonnage than any other, generating a quarter of Britain's imports; and better than half the world's international trade passed through the claustrophobic, clogged financial district between the East End docks and the prosperous West End. Air travel was coming into its own as well, with London at the center of a network of airways making international travel fast and practical.

London, then as now, was the seat of government—

legislative, executive and judiciary, with the House of Lords the Empire's supreme court of appeal—as well as home to the royal capital . . . Buckingham Palace, Westminster Abbey, St. Paul's and even the Tower of London down the Thames, where heads no longer rolled and the crown jewels were under watch by guards (and tourists).

Education was well-represented by eminent grammar schools (Alleyns, Battersea) and fine public schools (St. Paul's, Westminster), while London University rivaled Cambridge and Oxford. There were museums—the British Museum and National Gallery were only the beginning of an impressive array—and theater that made New York's Broadway look like the shabby vaudeville it was, plus comedies and musicals representing home-grown vaudeville as gloriously tasteless as anything the Yanks could muster.

Of course, a London resident had a higher cost of living than elsewhere in the kingdom; but the standard of living was also high, and even during the Depression—quelled by an economy spurred on by imminent war—unemployment had been low. The East End still had its share of poverty, however, and some considered a Bolshevik revolution inevitable.

A greater and even more imminent threat seemed to be London itself—its vulnerability, its dense population in a relatively small area, its attraction to an enemy desirous of delivering a "knock-out blow" to a target seemingly primed for an aerial attack.

And as we know, the bombs did drop . . . and the city did endure.

This is one small story in that greater drama, the account of one brave woman in that brave city, who like that city survived with dignity . . .

. . . and of a murderer who did not.

February 9, 1942

The wartime blackout, imposed in September of '39, was a fact of life Londoners had long since learned to live with—streetlights off, vehicles turned into one-eyed monsters (with the remaining headlight wearing a shade), and either a blocking board or black curtain screening all windows. Officious air wardens, particularly in the early days, had been the bullies in charge of banishing all illumination. Now no one thought about it, really. Compliance was second nature.

The blackout was part and parcel of being at war— like the sandbags piled high along sidewalks, the vaguely animal-like barrage balloons hovering over the city (like the air wardens, well-inflated), the starkly cheerful airbrushed posters advising Londoners to "carry on" and "do their bit." Even the sentries at Buckingham Palace had swapped their bright red uni-

forms for dingy battle fatigues, and streetcorner bobbies had traded in their helmets for tin hats.

Over two years into the war now, it was difficult to remember a time when children played on the sidewalks (most kiddies had been evacuated early on), and when automobiles on the street were thick as flies and not scarce as hen's teeth—a time when the tabloids were longer than a few pages, and a sales clerk wrapped your package in precious paper.

The city, or at least its people, seemed shabby of late—the clothing drab in color, often threadbare, no matter what your social status; new clothing was a rarity in this town, and when you wore new togs, you felt vaguely ashamed. The drabness extended itself to buildings—broken windows had become the exception, not the rule, and few structures wore fresh coats of paint; it seemed lacking in taste, somehow, when neighboring structures were piles of rubble.

Not that the city allowed itself to be a dirty, dusty shambles—repairs were constant. On this typically overcast, coldly dreary Monday morning, the street and sidewalks dusted with snow, workmen were repairing potholes. The latter were not the fault of the Germans— the last major attack had been back in May, after all, on the tenth . . .

. . . a night no one living in London was likely to forget. The Thames at low ebb, the moon full, the Luftwaffe delivered the war's worst raid thus far—Westminster Abbey damaged, the Mint, the Tower, the Law Courts, the British Museum hit, even Big Ben's face had been scarred (though still tolling right on time), as fires raged . . . and more than three thousand Londoners lost their lives. . . .

A shattered city had trembled, dreading the next attack; but nothing came, not for months, and even then nothing to compare to the tenth of May. And as days turned to weeks and weeks to months, the sense that the Blitz might be (dare one say it?) over provided a desperation-tinged hope.

Not that the city was letting down. Small but punishing German raids did occasionally still occur, the all-too-familiar banshee warning again piercing the London air—particularly following an Allied raid, most particularly when the target had been Berlin.

And, so, sandbags and rationing and propaganda posters and of course the blackout continued.

But the shelters weren't being so widely used, in this lull in the Blitz; and even when bombs were raining on London, many had preferred to stay home and take their chances, rather than crawl into a privately owned (usually ensconced in a garden) Anderson shelter, two corrugated sheets of steel bolted at the top, stuck three feet into the earth, with a sheet-metal door, and protected by an earthen embankment. With no drainage, these shelters for six were a nightmare; between the rain and certain human needs, one well might prefer the relative dignity of staying home and being blown to smithereens.

Then there was the public standard shelter of brick-and-lime mortar walls, perched unsupported on a roadway, with a nine-inch reinforced concrete slab on top. The public had soon dubbed these sandwich shelters, because a blast could suck the shelter walls outward, turning the occupants into the meat between concrete and roadway slices.

The "tubes" of the subway system were adapted into shelters as well, but mosquitoes and fierce winds (sometimes cold, sometimes hot) eventually relegated that option to the homeless. Little societies had developed down there, and even though they could be relocated, these ragged bands preferred their new underground world.

A workman named Peter Rushing, age thirty-eight, lanky and hard-hewed, was running short on sand in his pothole-filling effort. He knew where to "borrow" some, easy enough. . . .

Brick shelters like this one had to be built in the streets; there was no room, was there, for a structure like this in Montague Place, in the Central London district of Marlyebone, whose long, straight streets and endless rows of stately buildings—occasionally disrupted by bombed-out patches, like absent teeth in an otherwise impressive smile—included scant room for gardens. This shelter—between Edgware Road and Baker Street (both of whose flats and high-class shops had largely been destroyed in 1940's raids)—was but one of hundreds lining London's streets, a spare cubicle with a seat built along one side. Nothing could be more ordinary.

And yet Peter Rushing discovered something—someone—quite extraordinary, when he ducked into the stall intending to nick some sand from an already spilled-open sandbag.

The woman was striking—what you would call handsome as opposed to beautiful, with short, dark, nicely coifed hair and good cheekbones. She was not seated on the bench; rather she lay sprawled on the roadway floor of the shelter, her clothing—white blouse, dark brown jacket, lighter brown skirt—disarrayed, up over long legs that had been darkened with a liquid product to give the impression of silk stockings.

Her eyes were open and staring blankly. She had been gagged with a silk scarf, but was not otherwise bound, her arms and hands and legs splayed. No purse seemed present, but items apparently dumped from a purse were scattered nearby—lipstick, compact, handkerchief, and such. An electric torch—the woman's presumably—lay a ways from the body, its dim beam casting a small yellow circle on the brick wall under the bench.

And for the first time since the Blitz had begun, Peter Rushing was truly frightened. What he was viewing was not the impersonal carnage of war, rather the wanton destruction of one human's life by another.

"Freddie!" he called. "Come 'ere, lad!"

Freddie Sangster, a short chubby bloke of twenty-odd, did not move quickly; he had a game leg that had kept him doing roadwork during wartime. But when he got there, Freddie was quick to say, "Blimey," and agree that one of them should stay with the corpse, and the other go for the coppers.

And being the younger, Freddie got to stay and keep the woman company.

The boy was sitting on the bench, hunched over, his hands folded, his eyes on the handsome quite dead *woman, watching her carefully, as if to make sure she didn't make a break for it.*

And in the meantime, Peter Rushing did make a break for it—rushing off to find the nearest telephone.

ONE

Scant Shelter

Detective Chief Inspector Edward Greeno, Criminal Investigation Division, Scotland Yard, answered the call.

Greeno was a tall, square-shouldered man with a bucket head and bulldog features, a ready all-knowing smile and small dark eyes that missed little. He was one of the hardest-nosed coppers in town, and knew it; an inveterate horseplayer, Greeno had been approached with more bribe offers than a good-looking dame got whistles.

But much to the consternation of London's gangsters, Greeno was as straight as he was tough.

He stepped from the police Austin, allowing his driver to go park it, and strode toward the crime scene in snapbrim and raincoat, like any good detective; but what was a fashion statement for American dicks was a necessity for the likes of Greeno: the rain here was no joke, even though today it was a whispering of snow.

The inspector was a veteran of the legendary Flying Squad—sometimes called the Sweeney (short for Sweeney Todd, in cockney rhyming slang)—which "flew" to crime scenes and took literal pursuit of villains. He had earned countless commendations from judges and Scotland Yard commissioners, and crime reporter Percy Hoskins had called him "the underworld's public enemy number one."

Now Greeno, with what he considered to be a rather burdensome reputation, was attached to the Murder Squad—as it was unofficially known—though, unlike many chief inspectors, he had not during his sergeant days assisted on murder investigations.

Accordingly, Ted Greeno had only been investigating murders for a little over a year, and in wartime London, murders had been few. Crime was down all over London, actually.

In Greeno's view, there was nothing patriotic about it: a villain in peacetime was a villain in wartime. But with fewer motor cars around to nick, fewer got nicked; burglary was way down as well, since the blackout deterred crims, who had no way to know if a house or building was empty or not. Street violence, with an eye on robbery, was up, however—blackout bashing for cash seldom turned the corner into murder, though.

This was an apparent exception to that rule.

He had called for Sir Bernard Spilsbury to meet him at the scene of the crime. The renowned pathologist was on twenty-four hour call for the C.I.D., officially attached to the Home Office, although he worked not out of Scotland Yard but University College Hospital. The good doctor was not here as yet.

After he stepped through the narrow, doorless passageway in the high brick shelter walls, the inspector touched nothing. He did kneel over the dead woman and noted the state of her clothing's disarray . . . and the absence of a handbag. The purple bruises made by fingers on her throat were obvious even in the dimness of the shelter.

Had some thief strangled this woman over the contents of her bag? Had a few shillings cost this handsome woman her life?

Oddly, a fairly expensive-looking gold watch remained on the woman's wrist. Perhaps in the darkness the murderous thief had missed it.

Greeno would do little but wait until Sir Bernard was on hand. Confident as he might be about his skills as a police detective, Greeno knew that Spilsbury's expertise—and his eventual ability to testify in court with clarity and convincingness—was worth waiting for.

But something tingled at the back of the detective's neck—and in the pit of his stomach, a flutter of recognition. This corpse recalled another. . . .

One of the relative handful of murders in recent months had been that of Maple Church, an attractive young woman found strangled and robbed in a wrecked building on Hampstead Road.

And this attractive woman had obviously been robbed; and strangled.

Greeno was standing outside the shelter, questioning the two workmen, when Sir Bernard drew up in his dark-green Armstrong-Siddeley saloon; characteristically, Spilsbury had driven himself. With the exception of the sedan itself—motor cars a relative rarity these days—the pathologist's arrival was typically unobtrusive.

The man considered by many to be the first medical detective of modern times was accompanied by no retinue of assistants. His tall figure rather bent these days, his athletic leanness giving way to the plump spread of late middle age, Spilsbury—wearing no topcoat over a well-tailored dark suit with a carnation providing a bloodred splash in his otherwise somber attire—remained a striking, strikingly handsome figure.

Though his hair was silver now, and he was never seen without his wire-rimmed glasses, Sir Bernard Spilsbury had a matinee idol's chiseled features, highlighted by melancholy gray eyes that seemed to look at everything, but reluctantly, and a thin line of a mouth that with minimal change could suggest sorrow, disgust, reproach and even amusement.

The Crippen case—one of the century's most notorious—had marked Spilsbury's entry into the world of forensics; and over the intervening years no professional ups and downs had followed for Spilsbury, strictly what a wag had called "a steady climb to Papal infallibility."

Still, like so many in Britain, Spilsbury had not been spared by the war; his son Peter, a surgeon, had died in 1940, at the height of the Blitz. Greeno had heard the whispers: on that day, Sir Bernard had begun to fail.

His work, however, remained impeccable. It was

characteristic of Spilsbury to work alone in a politely preoccupied fashion. But his considerable charm, his dry wit, seemed to have evaporated. The touch of sadness in his eyes had spread to his solemn features.

"Doctor," Greeno said.

Greeno knew not to call Spilsbury "Sir Bernard" here; the pathologist considered that out of place at a crime scene.

"Inspector," Spilsbury said. He was lugging the almost comically oversize Gladstone bag that was his trademark. Then the pathologist raised one eyebrow and tilted his head toward the brick shelter.

Greeno nodded.

And this was the extent of the inspector briefing the pathologist.

Greeno followed Spilsbury through the narrow doorless doorway into the brick structure. The pathologist knelt beside the dead woman, as if he were praying; perhaps he was—one could never be sure about what might be going on in Sir Bernard's mind.

Then Spilsbury snapped the big bag; it yawned open gapingly to reveal various odd and old instruments, including probing forceps of his own invention, various jars and bottles (some empty, some full), and a supply of formalin. Also, he withdrew rubber gloves from somewhere within, which he snugged on.

Not all pathologists went the rubber-glove route. But Greeno knew Spilsbury—unlike many who should've known better—could be trusted to touch nothing at this crime scene other than the body, and even then with gloved fingertips. Any other evidence gathered by the pathologist would be preceded by a request to the detective in charge—in this case, Greeno.

The gloom of the shelter required Spilsbury to withdraw, from the seemingly bottomless bag, an electric torch, which he held in his right hand, using his left for other examinations. The pathologist was adeptly ambidextrous.

Never rising, Spilsbury started at the woman's feet and, bathing her selectively in the torch's yellow glow, closely looked at the clothed corpse as carefully as an actor studying his curtain speech. There was no rushing the doctor, although his methodical approach was diligent, not laggard.

It was Spilsbury, after all, who had taught Greeno that "clues can be destroyed through delay, and changes in the body after death . . . and the body's removal from where it was found . . . can confuse the medical evidence."

"With your permission," Spilsbury said, "I'm going to remove this watch."

"Please," Greeno said.

"I'll hold on to it, if I might."

"Do."

"I will pass it along to Superintendent Cherrill for fingerprint analysis and other testings."

"Fine."

Carefully, the rubber gloves apparently causing him no problem, Spilsbury removed the watch from the dead woman's wrist. He turned it over.

"We may have just identified the poor woman," Spilsbury said. "Take a look."

Spilsbury held the item up and Greeno leaned down.

On the back of the timepiece was engraved: *E.M. Hamilton.*

"It's not a cheap watch," Greeno said. "Odd our man left it behind, when he took her purse."

"Dark in here," Spilsbury said, making the same assumption Greeno had earlier. "He may simply have missed it."

The doctor was placing the watch in a small jar; this he labeled with a pen. Greeno knew material evidence was safe and sound in Spilsbury's keeping—whenever a case on which Spilsbury had worked came to court, the chain of possession of the evidence was flawless . . . only the great man himself and the laboratory analyst would have handled the stuff.

"*On such and such a date,*" the familiar testimony went, "*I was handed so many jars by Sir Bernard Spilsbury. . . .*"

Spilsbury's mournful, chiseled countenance looked up at Greeno. "Have you taken photographs?"

"One of my men has, yes."

"Then I'm going to unbutton her blouse, and may need to remove or undo an undergarment. Please block the doorway so that we're not interrupted."

Greeno did.

Finally, Spilsbury sighed as he rose, taking off the rubber gloves. He indicated the corpse, whose rather full breasts were exposed, though the pathologist largely obstructed Greeno's view. "I'd like more photographs, please."

Greeno made that happen, and briefly flashbulbs worked their lightning in the little space, strobing the corpse white.

Then the inspector and the pathologist were again alone with the victim. With Greeno's permission, Spilsbury took a sample of sand from a spilled sandbag, and placed individually the scattered items from the woman's missing purse into small manila envelopes. All of these potential exhibits disappeared into the massive Gladstone bag.

The pathologist took no notes. It was his practice not to impair the keenness of his senses with the distraction of note-taking, and would not do so until later, sometimes as much as days hence. Greeno was not disturbed by this: he knew Spilsbury wouldn't forget a damned thing.

"I'll leave the silk scarf for you to collect, Inspector."

"All right."

"Do be sure you have a photograph of the knot before it's undone."

"I will."

Spilsbury, who had tucked his rubber gloves away in that magician's bag, now stood and ritualistically placed his hands in his pants pockets—as he always did, once his medical examination was finished at a crime scene.

"Strangled, of course," Spilsbury said. "But you knew that."

"I prefer hearing it from you, Doctor."

"From the marks on her throat . . ." Spilsbury removed his left hand from his pocket, and held it out in a

choking manner, by way of demonstration. ". . . I believe her assailant was a left-handed man."

"You rule out a woman attacker?"

"It's unlikely. This is a powerful individual—much
more likely a male. On the other hand, despite the disarray of her clothing, I see no sign of rape or sexual attack. The autopsy will tell, of course."

"Of course."

Spilsbury nodded down toward the corpse. "Note the
bruises on her chest. . . . Come closer."

Greeno did and winced. "My God . . ."

"He probably knelt on top of her, pinning her down,
while he was strangling her."

The inspector shook his head. "It's a right wicked
world, Doctor."

"It is indeed. . . . Are you thinking what I'm thinking?"

Spilsbury had been at the Hampstead Road crime
scene, as well.

". . . Dare we think that?" Greeno asked.

"The other young woman, Maple Church," Spilsbury said, and the older man's ability to recall the name
was no surprise to the younger one, "was also strangled
and robbed. But, in that instance, there had been sexual
activity."

"Not rape, though."

Spilsbury nodded. "No evidence of such, anyway.
But sexual congress did occur, perhaps with the young
woman's consent."

Perhaps was an understatement, even for Spilsbury.
Maple Church had been a prostitute in Soho. Several

hours before her death, she'd been seen talking to potential mugs (as the London ladies called their clients)
not far from where her body would shortly be found.
Several service men had been on hand, among them
American soldiers.

"I don't believe any suspects made themselves available," Spilsbury said, drawing a fine line between tact
and sarcasm.

"We didn't get anywhere on that one, no, sir. With so
many servicemen in the city, it's difficult to impossible,
sometimes. . . . But if we would happen to have a boyo
who's preying upon prosties, this woman . . ." He nodded toward the austere-featured victim. ". . . would
hardly seem to qualify. She's handsome enough, but
rather old for the game."

"This was a respectable woman," Spilsbury said,
agreeing but in a dismissive manner. "Her clothing at-
tests that . . . but in a blackout, a woman walking the
street. . . . and she was, as you say, handsome. . . ."

"He could easily have mistaken her for a tart."

Spilsbury nodded curtly. "But two killings don't a
Ripper make."

"No. These could be isolated instances. Robberies
gone out of hand."

"In hand, I should say," Spilsbury said, repeating the
choking gesture. "I would hate to think the fog of
Whitechapel has a counterpart in our blackouts."

Greeno grunted a humorless laugh. "That's where I
started out, you know."

Spilsbury looked at Greeno directly, as if noticing
his presence for the first time. "What's that, Inspector?"

"King David's Lane, Shadwell—Whitechapel Division. That was my first post, back in '20. Where the Ripper ripped."

"I pray we don't have another."

"Second to that. And if we do . . . I pray he's not American."

Spilsbury's eyes and nostrils flared. "Oh—that would be all we'd need at this juncture."

The influx of American soldiers since the first of the year had been considerable . . . as was the tension between locals and the colonials. The phrase going around of late was "the Americans are over-paid, over-sexed and over here." The Home Office, it was rumored, was developing a campaign to convince British citizens that the Americans were not pampered, gum-chewing, arrogant monsters.

Somehow Greeno doubted an American Jack the Ripper would do much to advance that campaign.

Spilsbury packed up—no one was allowed to touch his fabled "murder" bag, and in fact the pathologist would give a frighteningly reproving glare to any person who dared touch even his sleeve at a crime scene—and took his leave, the Armstrong-Siddeley disappearing into the snowy morning.

And soon Greeno was out on the street, in front of the shelter.

A plainclothes policeman—not a policeman in plainclothes (the latter received an extra 5s. a week for wear and tear)—came rushing up, holding a woman's handbag.

"Guv'nor!" the ruddy-cheeked cop called. "Take a gander!"

"Goes nicely with your eyes, Albert."

Albert, who was a trifle heavyset, was breathing hard, his breath in fact smoking in the chill. "You won't be pullin' my leg when I tell you what this is, Guv."

"It's our victim's handbag."

"Right on the bleedin' button, Guv. Found 'er on top of a trashbin in the alley, there, I did. I think we know who our unfortunate shelter sleeper is."

"Her last name's Hamilton."

The copper's eyes widened. "Sexton Blake's got nothin' on you, Guv. Evelyn Hamilton. There's no wallet, but a receipt for a night's lodging was tucked down in."

"Which gives us an address to check."

"It does."

The address took Greeno to Oxford Street; few major London thoroughfares had suffered as much damage as Oxford, with many buildings new and old turned to so much rubble. To the inspector perhaps the saddest loss of all was Buszard's famous cake-shop, a landmark for a hundred years till a two-in-the-morning bomb destroyed the facade as well as the Palm Court where grand teas had not long ago been served. As he glided by the remains in his Austin, he savored sweet memories of sweets. . . .

The four-story lodging house was an ironically shabby survivor among distinguished casualties, and its landlady, a haggard hatchet-faced harridan in a faded housedress, stood leaning on a broom in a doorway giving Greeno chapter and verse. She had tiny eyes, Greeno thought; piss holes in the snow.

"Not safe on these streets for a decent woman," she

said, in a voice reminiscent of an air-raid siren. "There's blackout muggers on them streets I tell you, and what are you police doin' about it? It's them Yanks, y'know."

"Miss Hamilton was a decent woman, then?"

"Salt of the earth. She was manager of a pharmacy till last week. She give notice. Are you afraid to haul these American blighters in? Make too many waves, will it?"

"Do you know why Miss Hamilton gave notice? At the pharmacy?"

"Well, she was a teacher, you see, and with so many schools closed now, she took that job at the chemist's, out of necessity, don't you know. But a teaching position opened up, up North—Grimsby way."

"Did she have gentleman friends?"

"No, poor thing—she was a shy one. A regular spinster lady. Oh, she'd wear a touch of make-up, like to make herself presentable."

"Maybe she had one special gentleman, then?"

"Not while she was stayin' here. Spent most of her spare time alone in her room—reading them books on chemistry of hers, I'd wager."

"Does it seem to you likely she'd have allowed herself to be picked up by a strange man?"

"Miss Hamilton! Not on your life. She never spoke to no one unless she was introduced. . . . Don't you be blackening that good woman's name, now! It's one of them Americans what grabbed her—mark my word! If you were to have more coppers on the street during the blackout—"

"Thank you ma'am. Can you think of anything else that might be pertinent?"

Tiny eyes grew tinier. "Well—she had quite a sum of money on her."

Greeno frowned in interest. "Is that right?"

"Oh, blimey, yes. She settled accounts with me, cash, just last evening—if you check her room, you'll find her bags packed. She was to take the train to Grimsby today."

"And she was traveling with money?"

"Eighty pounds, I'd say. I call that money. Small fortune, by me."

So Evelyn Hamilton hadn't been killed for "a few shillings," then. Eighty pounds in wartime London was a small fortune indeed.

The inspector followed up with interviews at the pharmacy, manager and co-workers, which confirmed the landlady's characterization of the dead woman. Interviews with acquaintances and others in the lodging house painted the same picture: the victim was a spinster schoolteacher, proper, reticent. One friend did say Miss Hamilton had dated a teacher at a school several years ago, and suspected she was joining her old beau up north at this new post.

Greeno would check that.

By late afternoon a Marlyebone seafood restaurant was confirmed as the last location where anyone (other than her killer) had seen Evelyn Margaret Hamilton alive. The cashier reported seeing the wad of pound notes in the woman's purse.

She'd been handsome enough to attract a sexual predator, Greeno thought; but that cash would have been attractive to most any villain.

Greeno could see it in his mind's eye: *during the blackout, the attractive schoolteacher walks from the restaurant back to her lodgings; along the way, a man tries to grab the purse, and when she struggles, he drags her into the nearby air-raid shelter and silences her.*

Not a twentieth-century Jack the Ripper. Just a mugger who had let his crime get a little out of hand.

And yet those disarrayed clothes, and that the crim had taken time to gag the woman indicated that he had intended, at least, to take his time . . . and perhaps have his way with the woman.

Something had spooked the assailant, other folks out walking in the blackout most likely, and he had strangled the woman and taken her eighty pounds and left her there, lifeless, on the sandy floor of the shelter.

And if the villain had been interrupted, when he'd meant to have his way with the schoolteacher . . . well, that troubled Inspector Ted Greeno most of all.

Because villains liked to be satisfied.

TWO

Prescription: Murder

The buildings of University College Hospital, on Gower Street in Bloomsbury, intersected in the form of a cross, but this had not discouraged the Germans from bombing it—perhaps it had only provided a better target. At any rate, several of the buildings had been badly damaged in the air raids of 1940, and there were flattened buildings all around; and yet the hospital itself was largely standing, clean-up long since complete, though reconstruction was going slowly.

The dispensary, where Mrs. Mallowan worked two full days, three half-days (often evenings) and alternate Saturday mornings, was untouched, and remained quite the orderly rabbit's warren it had always been. Rather like the library of a country village, whose stacks were devoted to pills not books, the dispensary was home to four dispensers (two at a time) and one Sealyham terrier.

His white sausage-like form stretched out under the shelves, the terrier was a small, short-legged, long-headed, strong-jawed, whiskered white lamb of a dog called James who belonged to Mrs. Mallowan's long-time secretary, Carlo Fisher. Sometimes Mrs. Mallowan thought she missed Carlo's presence as much as that of Mr. Mallowan (a gross exaggeration) (she thought) (she hoped), as Carlo was working in a munitions factory now and was unable to have James with him. So Mrs. Mallowan had adopted the dog for the duration.

James behaved impeccably at the hospital and there had been no complaints about his behavior, and he received occasional kind attentions from the charwoman, as well as from the several dispensers with whom Mrs. Mallowan shared these cramped quarters.

Of the dispensers, all five were female and of these Mrs. Mallowan was quite the senior, if in reality the least experienced, or at any rate the one who'd only recently qualified in the up-to-date medicines and tonics and ointments and such, prescribed nowadays. The chief dispenser, a serious slender woman, thirty-odd, with Harold Lloyd eyeglasses, often paused to make sure Mrs. Mallowan was "getting it right."

Which was quite ridiculous, as on the whole, working in a dispensary was much easier these days than in Mrs. Mallowan's younger ones. In a modern dispensary, so many pills, tablets, powders and things were already waiting in bottles or tubes or otherwise prepackaged, requiring little to none of the skill of measuring and mixing the profession once demanded; she really did seem a sort of librarian of medicines.

Mrs. Mallowan felt somewhat ill at ease, even self-conscious among these younger women. Though she would never have been so rude or bold to say so, the volunteer worker knew very well that, when she was their age, in her twenties, she would have put them to shame.

She had been a willowy young thing, a tall, slim blonde with thick, wavy, waist-long hair, delicate skin, sloping shoulders, and the half-lidded blue eyes, gently aquiline nose and oval face consistent with the Edwardian ideal of feminine beauty.

Even in her housewifely thirties (early thirties, at any rate), she could have held her own.

Now, in her white lab coat, she still struck a commanding figure, taller than these youngsters, and not yet . . . the word came slowly but inexorably . . . fat. Her waist had vanished, it was true, and she had one more chin than she felt really necessary, a formidable drooping bosom bequeathed her by her late beloved mother, and the sun-kissed fair hair had turned a gunmetal gray which she wore short, a cap of curls providing an unexceptional accompaniment to features no longer lovely (in her view), comprising what could only charitably be described as a "kind" face.

She was resigned to her new lot in life. At fifty-two she no longer viewed herself as "middle-aged"—not unless she would live to be a hundred and four, and she had no real desire of that—and yet the dreaded half-century mark had been a liberation of sorts. She had experienced a renewed verve for living, that heightened sense of awareness only years can bring; she found that she enjoyed going to picture shows, concerts and the opera with the same enthusiasm as when she'd been twenty or twenty-five.

Her marriage to Max—could it really be a dozen years ago?—had made the difference. The emotional turmoil of romantic personal relations had been replaced by the contentment of loving, harmonious companionship. With Max, she could enjoy her leisure time—travel to foreign places at the forefront, of course.

Not that the bedroom was a dull place with Max—encounters between the sheets remained a pleasure not a duty; this was one of the positive aspects of being married to a man fourteen years younger than yourself (though the weight she was putting on in his absence did trouble her).

And what a pleasure too that those infantile cat-and-mouse courtship games were ancient history (what a ghastly tedious disappointment it had been, after her first marriage had ended, to discover the courtship rituals for those in their thirties and forties differed so little from those in their teens and twenties).

Only now she and Max were separated by this war, this damned war. And here she was, back in a hospital dispensary, where she'd been in the last one. Not that history was repeating itself—the "war to end all wars" had been different, coming as it did as an incomprehensible shock, a cataclysm unlike anything in living memory, the impossible happening.

No, this conflict was quite different, even if it was the Germans again. This time the surprise came from how long the war took to really truly start. Like so many others, the Mallowans—who had heard the proclamation of war broadcast on the kitchen radio while the household help wept into the vegetables—had expected London to be bombed that first night; but nothing happened.

When nothing kept on happening, the country got itself organized, more or less, sitting waiting for disaster to inflict itself . . . which it refused to do. And so, with the war remaining a concept and not a reality, the country slipped back into individual pursuits, mundane daily life, interspersed with occasional wartime activities, such as when Max joined the comic opera that was the Brixham Home Guard, ten men passing around two rifles.

Embarrassed by such pointless activities, Max had gone off to London, to the Air Ministry, hoping to be sent abroad on a mission. Greenway—their newly acquired but much loved home on the river Dart, between Torquay and Dartmouth—had been requisitioned as a nursery for evacuated London children, though Mrs. Mallowan continued to live there for a time.

That was what had taken her back to the Torquay dispensary, where she'd picked up an on-the-job refresher course which had made her current University College posting possible.

When her first husband, Archie, was serving with the Royal Flying Corps, she had worked as a volunteer nurse and then as a hospital dispensing pharmacist. Nursing during the Great War had been a nasty bit of business—from the rigors of constantly cleaning the wards and scrubbing rubber sheets to attending to burn patients and assisting in the operating room, the job was not for the easily fatigued or the faint of heart.

Pampered ladies with romantic notions of soothing our brave boys' fevered brows did not last long—not after tidying up following amputations and disposing severed limbs in the hospital furnace, they didn't. Mrs. Mallowan had lasted fifteen months, and might have stayed longer, but a dose of flu instigated by overwork, and the attraction of more regular hours, had brought her to the dispensary.

There she found a calm seldom present in nursing; difficult at first, the dispensing job played well into her natural interest in, and facility with, mathematics. Codifying, classifying, listing, measuring, learning symbols and signs, mastering the appearance and properties of various substances . . . this was a kind of poetry to her.

And the dispensary was a life-and-death operation, no less than an operating room—she had seen a confident if careless pharmacist prepare a mixture based upon a calculation that was one decimal point off. Rather than embarrass the man (and kill some unwitting patient), she had spilled the mixture and endured censure for clumsiness . . . .

Still, interesting as dispensing was, she found it rather monotonous—ointments, medicines, jar after jar of lotions to be filled and refilled, day after day. She should never have cared for dispensing as a permanent job, and had her life gone a different way, she might have been happy to remain a professional nurse.

But it was in the pharmacy that Mrs. Mallowan had picked up a working knowledge of poisons, and this personal experience she used in the writing of her first mystery novel, *The Mysterious Affair at Styles*.

Ironically, the boring if sociable dispensary (she'd worked there with two good friends) set her mind to wandering, looking for escape from the anxiety of wartime in the form of daydreams that led to the notion of writing a mystery based upon a notably ingenious way to slip poison to a victim. . . .

And now Agatha Christie Mallowan found herself back in a dispensary, with her mind running down a similar and yet distinctively different course. She was well aware that her mystery novels were of a polite, even cozy nature—superficially, at least—and even reflective of another era.

She did not like to think of herself as old-fashioned; and she had tried, in her work, to do things no writer of mysteries had ever dared—the narrator is the killer, all the suspects did it, a child, the love interest, even the detective himself might be the murderer. Puzzles, they called her stories, and she would smile and nod; but Agatha knew her tales of good and evil hinged on character.

In her way, Agatha was an innovator, and she had of late begun to wonder if the cataclysm of this war would result in a post-war world whose innocence was so lost that bodies in libraries and detectives exercising little gray cells would seem quaintly out of step and, well, just too ridiculous.

Her morning's last customer (was it terrible to think of them that way?) was a tiny old Irish lady, remindful of Mother Riley from the music hall, who handed over her prescription with one hand and pressed half a crown into Agatha's palm with the other.

In a wrinkled leprechaun face, blue eyes twinkled, and then one of them winked. "Make it double strong, dearie, will you now? Plenty of peppermint, my darling girl—double strong!"

"We don't accept bribes," Agatha said priggishly, returning the half-crown.

A frown wrinkled the wizened face further. "I would never insult you that way, dearie. T'ink of it as a gratuity. A gift."

"You will receive exactly the dosage your doctor prescribed," Agatha said stiffly, but when she turned her back, the dispenser allowed the smile she'd been stifling to blossom. She mixed in an extra dollop of peppermint water for the old girl—it could not possibly do her any harm—and then pretended to be stern when she handed it over.

Her half-day ended at noon, at which time she hung up her lab coat, to reveal her off-white blouse and the dark gray skirt of her well-made, respectable Debenham and Freebody suit. Her stockings were black and warm, her shoes heavy and sensible. She slipped into the gray suitjacket, slung her well-lined Burberry over an arm, attached the leash to James's collar, and she and the terrier made their familiar way to the small laboratory just down the hall from the dispensary.

Within this glorified cubbyhole—workbench beneath a window overlooking the courtyard, sink and rack of test tubes nearby, counter with bunsen burners beneath specimen-lined shelves—the greatest forensics scientist of the twentieth century kept solitary company with his investigations.

When Agatha had first heard that Sir Bernard Spilsbury was her neighbor at University College Hospital, a schoolgirl giddiness ran through her. She had read and heard much about Sir Bernard, and the idea of meeting him, of discussing with him crime and murder and poisons and causes of death, frankly thrilled her.

But she had never made the journey down the hall to introduce herself. Agatha was not outgoing, at least not until she got to know a person; this reticence prevented her from making the immediate acquaintance of someone she had much admired, from afar.

She understood that Sir Bernard, too, was shy and unassuming, amazingly so for so well-known a public figure; like her, he was said to abhor attention, and despised having his picture taken. In the hallways of the hospital, she had observed him discreetly—he seemed distracted though never rude, preoccupied but nonetheless likable, displaying charm and even warmth when someone on the staff stopped to make conversation with him.

Certainly she needn't fear offending him; and yet she could not bring herself to make an introduction—how silly she would feel, the author of homicidal confections presenting herself to the man who put Crippen away.

And yet she had longed to meet him. It was almost—but not quite—as if she were a schoolgirl with a crush. Certainly, even in his mid-sixties, Sir Bernard cut a handsome figure—always in a dark well-tailored suit with a fresh carnation, a tall figure understandably thickened at the middle, with the sharply chiseled features of a matinee idol, and eyes as grey as Poirot's little brain cells.

Perhaps, with Max away, there was an element of propriety afoot as well. Agatha had not known how to approach this handsome, older man she so admired without fawning, even gushing, and perhaps giving him . . . the wrong idea.

Then, finally, he had introduced himself—not at the hospital, but inside Euston Station.

Euston Station, of course, was an undeniably shabby affair, inconvenient, shambling, with a cavernous entrance hall cutting the station in two and encouraging bedlam. She disliked crowds, hated being jammed up against people, and the loud sounds and the cigarette and cigar smoke all annoyed her; but wartime was wartime, wasn't it? One did what one had to do.

And so Agatha—who so loved to eat, who so adored fine cooking, by herself and others—had been reduced to taking bangers and mash at a stall, sitting at a little wooden table whose secondary function seemed to be providing irony that a hospital worker should eat at so unsanitary a spot. James the terrier would curl up on the floor beside her, waiting for an occasional bite of banger to reward his good behavior.

She had noticed Sir Bernard taking an occasional lunch here, sitting engrossed in a book or writing in a journal; so it was not a surprise to see him approaching, typically natty in a dark suit, set off by a red carnation in the buttonhole, raincoat over his arm.

It was, however, a shock for him to stop and half-bow before her, even as she did her best to swallow a rather too-large bite of mashed potatoes.

"Pardon me, Mrs. Mallowan," he had said, his voice a rich baritone, "I'm Bernard Spilsbury. Might I sit down for a moment?"

"Please! Please do."

He did. "Forgive my forwardness. I just recently learned that you were assisting in the University pharmacy, and I very much wanted to meet you."

Suddenly Agatha felt a wave of disappointment: could the great forensics expert really just be another enthusiast? Another fan eager to meet "the mistress of mystery?"

Where most authors might be flattered, this was an embarrassment to Agatha, and caused in her an immediate diminishment of respect for Sir Bernard.

From the day she'd taken her post at the pharmacy, she had made it clear to all and sundry that she was "Mrs. Mallowan," not "Agatha Christie," not on those premises. That she was not to be bragged about or paraded around for the amusement of patients and/or doctors. She would be happy to sign a book for anyone in the pharmacy, should they so desire. But after that she preferred to disappear into her role: Mrs. Mallowan, assistant dispenser.

Sir Bernard was gazing over his wire-framed glasses at her; he seemed a little embarrassed himself as he worked his soft voice above the clangs of the trains and the clamor of the crowd. "You see, Mrs. Mallowan . . . I'm a great admirer . . ."

Here it comes, she thought, *with the endless questions about where one gets one's ideas, and how could a kind-looking woman like you devise such diabolical . . .*

". . . of your husband," Sir Bernard was saying.

She rocked back, flushed with surprise and pleasure. "Really? Of Max?"

"Oh yes, Mrs. Mallowan." The chiseled features were softened with admiration as he shook his head. "Archaeology is a hobby for which, necessarily, I've had less and less time as I've gotten older."

"Archaeology," Agatha said, beaming. "Oh yes. Isn't it simply wonderful?"

He nodded. "My son Peter used to point out that archaeology rallied my detective's instincts."

"Ah." She too nodded. "In pathology you must answer the same question posed in archaeology: 'What happened in the past to leave evidence in the present?' "

Now Sir Bernard beamed. "Almost Peter's words exactly."

She wondered if Peter was the son she had heard Sir Bernard had lost, in the air raids of 1940.

"Mr. Mallowan's excavations at Ur with Leonard Wooley," Sir Bernard was saying, "are legendary. And then his digs in Ninevah, Iraq, Syria . . . how exciting. How terribly romantic."

She smiled. "I don't know that sorting and listing artifacts, and cleaning arrowheads and pottery shards with face cream, is 'terribly romantic,' nor exciting, exactly . . . but I did love it."

The grey eyes flared with interest. "I understood you accompanied your husband from time to time! You're to be commended."

"I shouldn't be commended for doing something I so enjoy. Away from our so-called civilization . . . blessedly free from the press and the public. I do some of my best writing in the desert."

"Yes, I understand you're a writer."

Her pleasure waned, suddenly; it was wonderful for Sir Bernard to be an admirer of Max's, and a relief not to be dealing with a fawning fan.

And yet this was, somehow, a disappointment . . . that Sir Bernard knew so little of her, and what she did, and who she was.

She touched the side of her head, fingers in the curls. "I must say Max's work resembles mine, as well. Stories of crime and murder can be uncovered in the ancient sands."

"I must apologize for not being acquainted with your work," Sir Bernard said. Perhaps he had sensed her bruised pride. "I understand your reputation is considerable . . . and many of my colleagues read mystery and detective stories. For my part, I have no interest in fictional crime. . . . I hope I haven't offended you."

"Not at all," she said, and her hurt had vanished. "It would be a busman's holiday for you, wouldn't it?"

"As I'm afraid I've revealed, I'm secretly a romantic—Tennyson, Wordsworth, Kipling, those are my literary heroes."

"You display impeccable taste, Sir Bernard."

"Please, Mrs. Mallowan. I'd be honored if you'd call me Bernard."

"Only if you'll call me Agatha."

He shifted in his seat. "If you want me to . . . Agatha . . . I'll read one of your books. . . ."

She laughed, a rather raucous laugh that gave her a twinge of chagrin. "That's not necessary . . . Bernard. Have you had lunch? Would you care to join me?"

"That's very kind of you."

And he did, ordering up his own plate of bangers and mash.

Thereafter they had lunch together almost every weekday, as her schedule and his work allowed. His wife Edith was living out of London, and Sir Bernard saw her only on occasional weekends. Agatha—lonely herself, without Max—could sense the man's need for companionship.

This was no love affair—far from it. This was simply two older people whose spouses were away, two professionals pursuing their careers during wartime, as best they could, who found pleasure in each other's company. Now and then they ate at the stall in Euston Station, but more often at the Holborn.

Sir Bernard asked endless questions about Max's archaeological digs, and seemed far more impressed with Agatha's role as expedition photographer, complete with darkroom tent, than her status as an author of bestselling mystery novels.

"It's wonderful to be married to an archaeologist," she told Sir Bernard. "The older you get, the more interested he is in you."

People who knew them both as painfully shy individuals probably wondered if the pair of them had lost their minds, these two reticent types sitting chattering like magpies. But they had much in common, including a love of music; she revealed to Sir Bernard her failed ambition to be an opera singer (her voice had proved too thin, and incipient stage fright had been no help, either) and he told her almost misty-eyed of his days as a medical student attending Henry Wood's promenade concerts.

They had become good enough friends to allow the other silence—there were days when she was troubled by difficulties with her writing (she had plenty of time for that in the evenings—one didn't want to go out in the Blitz!). And she would sit and quietly think and their conversation would be politely minimal.

When he was preoccupied with a case, Sir Bernard could lapse into intense silence, often checking a small black spiral notebook filled with file-size note cards, as if life were an exam for which he was studying.

As she (and James on his leash) entered the little lab down the hall at the hospital, Sir Bernard sat at a counter in his white lab coat, his brow furrowed as he went over those ubiquitous file cards in his little black notebook.

"Good afternoon, Bernard," she said, as was her habit.

He looked up, his smile a barely noticeable crease under the intense grey eyes and finely carved nose. "Is it afternoon already?" he replied, as was his wont.

And soon they had walked, quietly, to nearby Holborn Empire, once known as the Royal Theater of Varieties (and badly damaged by a bomb in 1941). At the west corner of Kingsway, the Holborn restaurant welcomed them; in the last century it was the largest dance hall in London. Now it was a largely male bastion of dark luxuriant wood and waiters who spoiled Sir Bernard with special dishes despite wartime rationing. Agatha doubted Sir Bernard—whose egalitarian treatment of these waiters over the years had no doubt inspired this uninvited loyalty—was at all aware of this favoritism.

The steak-and-kidney pie luncheon was as wordless as it was delicious, and—as they both took coffee afterward—Agatha said, "You must be on a case. You seem terribly preoccupied."

"Yes. Nasty bit of business."

"We've never discussed any of your cases."

"No. I suppose we haven't."

"Some people might find that . . . odd."

"Really, Agatha. And why is that?"

She cocked her head, raised an eyebrow. "You are, after all, the foremost forensics expert in Great Britain."

He just looked at her; no false modesty prompted any need to comment.

"And I," she said, and trailed off.

But he said nothing.

She sighed. "And *I* am the foremost author of crime novels in Great Britain."

"I should say the world," he said casually.

This caught her off-guard. "You would? You really would?"

"I believe," he said, sipping his coffee through the parted lips of the faintest smile, "I just did."

A warm glow coursed through her, though she was a little ashamed that it had.

"At any rate," she said, "we have never discussed crime, have we? Or murder, or mystery."

"We have not. What did you call it? Busman's holiday?"

"Are you aware that I frequently use poison for my murders?"

His eyes opened wide. "Fictional murders, I trust."

"Fictional murders, yes. And you are one of the world's most renowned experts on poison as used in murder cases."

"One of . . . ?"

She laughed gently. "*The* most renowned. . . . There's a wonderful story about you. I wonder if it's true."

"You might ask."

"I have heard," she said, "that at the time of the Croydon poisonings, you arrived at the graveside dressed in your typically immaculate manner—right down to a top hat."

"That does sound like me."

"And when the coffin was raised, you leaned in, ran your nose along the side of the box, stood up straight and said, 'Arsenic, gentlemen.' "

She had hoped for a smile or another light remark, but instead a melancholy cast came over his features.

"Bernard—is something wrong?"

His voice was soft; almost faint—she had to work to hear it, over the clatter of dishes and table chatter.

"When was it . . . twenty years ago? I was working on a particularly unpleasant exhumation case. . . . Is this bothering you? We did just eat, after all, and I—"

"I have never been prone to squeamishness, Bernard."

". . . Well, there he was, all laid out, ready for examination. And the young C.I.D. officer on the case, standing beside me, possibly nervous at his first autopsy, fired up a cigarette! I turned to him sharply and said, 'Young man, you mustn't smoke. I won't be able to smell the smells I want to smell.' "

"And then," Agatha said gaily, "you bent down over the corpse and sniffed away . . . as if the deceased were a rose garden. . . . I've heard that story, too."

His face was blank and yet the distress was evident. "My sense of smell . . . it's almost gone."

She sat forward. "Oh, Bernard . . . how simply dreadful."

He shrugged, slightly. "And what I insist upon calling lumbago . . . but which we all know is severe arthritis . . . has settled in the low of my back, most cozily."

Her response was a flinch of a smile, followed by: "That's the penalty of age—but these things happen, Bernard, and must be endured. As I get older, the gift of life seems stronger, more vital . . ."

"Even in time of war?"

She chose her words carefully; she knew he had lost a son in the Blitz—Peter, as she had surmised at their first meeting. "In such times, in a world of broken windows and bombs and land mines, it's natural to expect that you yourself might be killed soon . . . that you will hear of the death of friends . . . that those you love best might be lost. . . ."

A humorless smirk twitched on one cheek. "But one must not despair, I suppose."

She shook her head. "One carries on. Not that one does not take . . . precautions."

Something like amusement glimmered in the grey eyes. "Whatever precautions might a renowned mystery writer take?"

She sat up straight and announced, "I have just completed my last two books."

"Your last . . . ?"

"I have written one final novel about my vile little Belgian, and have taken the utmost pleasure in killing him off, too! And I've just completed one last Jane Marple mystery, as well."

He sat forward. "You don't intend to stop writing, my dear. . . ."

She chuckled. "No. By my 'last' novels, I mean I've produced willfully posthumous novels—copies are in bank vaults here and in New York. These are a legacy of a sort, an insurance policy if you will, for my husband and daughter."

He sat back, smiling a relieved smile. "I must admit, the thought of you giving up writing seems unlikely to say the least."

She leaned an elbow on the table and rested her chin in a palm. "But the question is . . . what sort of writing will I pursue?"

"I don't follow. Won't you continue with mysteries and things?"

"There is a part of me that thinks those two novels should indeed be the last to feature that tired pair of out-of-date sleuths."

"Out of date . . . how so?"

"They are of another time. Poirot's world of upper-class Manor House shenanigans and Marple's world of country-cottage village treachery. Postcards from a more innocent era."

Sir Bernard's eyes narrowed. "As opposed to missives from a world of broken windows and bombs and land mines?"

"Precisely." She heaved a world-weary sigh. "I have moved more and more into espionage novels of late, and . . . am I boring you?"

"Do I seem bored?"

"Not at all . . . but I really would not like to—"

"Please, Agatha. I am privileged to be your father confessor."

She chuckled again. "Bernard, I wonder if in the postwar world . . . should this war ever end, and should we find ourselves living in a country where writers can publish something other than variations upon *Mein Kempf* . . . I wonder if my style of murder will still be in vogue?"

Now he was openly amused. "What other style of murder were you considering?"

"If you laugh at me, I'll throw a napkin at you. I swear I will."

He held up his hands in surrender. "I believe you. The question was serious."

She sighed. "So is the answer. . . . Are you aware of this new style of supposedly 'realistic' crime novel that's come out of the States?"

"No."

"Well, suffice to say there's a school known as the 'hardboiled'—"

"What a wretchedly unpleasant term."

"Isn't it? And the books themselves are rather wretchedly unpleasant, as well. One of them does write well—perhaps you've heard of him . . . Dashiell Hammett?"

"No."

"Former Pinkerton detective. He writes nicely compact prose. But his followers are for the most part blood-and-thunder practitioners—bloody violence, blatant sex. There's a fellow named Chandler who writes vividly, but his plots are incomprehensible rubbish . . . please don't quote me."

"You have my word."

"But, still and all, these writers may be onto something . . ."

"Something unpleasant, I should say."

"Indeed. They sense that the public . . . as the world around us grows ever more horrific . . . itself is growing numb, needing ever increasing stimuli. Whatever I might think of their writing, they point toward the modern world. An unpleasant world." She shuddered. "Can you imagine what the first big American crime writer, post-war, is likely to be like? What sort of unwashed brute will *he* be?"

Wisely, Sir Bernard left this rhetorical question unanswered. "I take it you are contemplating writing more realistically about crime and murder."

She nodded, narrowing her eyes. "Bernard, you've stated it far more simply and eloquently than has the paid professional writer."

"Thank you."

"The question is—will you help me?"

"How?"

She leaned close and held his eyes with hers. "I want to accompany you to crime scenes. I want to see how you work, and how the police work, and achieve a firmer grasp on the reality behind the fantasy I serve up."

He reared back. "Oh, Agatha, I don't know that that's a good idea."

"It's a splendid idea. Will you help?"

"I'm not so sure it can even be arranged."

"Bernard, if the most renowned mystery writer on the planet joins forces with the foremost forensics detective in the universe . . . how could it not?"

He just sat there, stunned for a moment, then smiled and laughed. "You are truly a one of a kind, Mrs. Mallowan."

"Thank you, Sir Bernard. Now, what is this case that's got you studying in your little black notebook so diligently?"

The smile dissolved into a frown. "I wouldn't advise starting there. It's a most unpleasant matter."

"Most murders are."

"We may have . . . I must ask your discretion."

"Certainly."

He whispered: "We may have a modern-day Jack the Ripper on our hands."

Agatha gasped. "Oh . . . that's wonderful."

Sir Bernard's eyes tightened; he looked frankly horrified.

Her heart sank. "Please, please don't think badly of me. . . . It's just that this is exactly the kind of case I'm craving. Something big . . . a multiple murderer. . . . It's just what the doctor ordered."

His eyes were very wide. "My dear . . . this is not your . . . 'fantasy' world. Now, sit back and I will tell you about the crime scene I visited this morning."

And he did. He even referred to his little black notebook, to make sure no details were omitted.

Agatha, feeling ashamed of herself, said, "I behaved wretchedly . . . selfishly. Poor woman. Her death is a tragedy, not just . . . research for some silly writer. Do forgive me."

"Then you'll give up this foolish idea?"

"Certainly not. It's perfect. And I would say that your assumption is correct, Bernard. This fiend will strike again."

He shook his head. "We're not even sure the two murders are in fact the work of one assailant."

"If it is the same man, you have to find him . . . and stop him. Because he isn't finished, you know."

A waiter stopped by to fill their coffee cups.

"I wish," Sir Bernard said, "I could say I disagree with you. . . . So what would you have me do, then? Call you if our Ripper strikes again? Take you along to the scene of the crime?"

She sipped her coffee; it was bitter, but there was no cream.

"Yes," Agatha said.

Ten minutes later, Agatha was leading James down the pavement with an obedient Sir Bernard at her side.

"You're certain you want to do this?" the pathologist asked.

"Quite."

"Aren't you busy working on this play of yours—*Ten Little Something-or-Others*?"

"Just finishing touches, darling," she said, the latter word an archly theatrical touch. "But you're right, I am busy. In fact, I'm not working at the hospital this afternoon—I'll be at the theater. The St. James? You can call me there, should anything arise."

They were clipping along, the terrier setting a quick pace, despite the crowded pavement (which ran past an all-but-deserted street).

Sir Bernard asked, "Doesn't the play open soon?"

"Yes. Friday. I've offered you tickets, several times. I could use the company—first nights are such agony for me."

"Perhaps we should wait until after Friday, for you to accompany me to any crime scene . . ."

She smiled innocently at him. "Do you think the Ripper will wait?"

He frowned. "Agatha, I have grave misgivings."

"Is that a pun?"

"How often do you have an opening night, my dear?"

"Bernard," she said with mild exasperation. "Every time you perform an autopsy, it's opening night."

And after that, apparently, Sir Bernard Spilsbury could think of nothing else to say on the subject.

THREE

Ten Little Actresses

The St. James Theatre, on King Street, was its usual majestic self, though the building next door, Willis Sale Rooms, was in a sorry state. This noted home of public dinners, meetings and cotillions had been severely damaged in the 1940 air raids; the sumptuous site, with its spacious supper room with gallery and ballroom, still tempted after-hours looters. The St. James was nonetheless structurally sound, despite its shambles of a nextdoor neighbor; and the pub on the other side of the theater, the Golden Lion, remained healthy, even if Christie's Auction House, across the way, was vacant due to bombing, as well. That the theater district resembled a war zone . . . in fact, was a war zone . . . did not deter the production of another Christie's work.

Right now the St. James bore a massive angled marquee adorned with both the author's name and that of the new play—a controversial title, it would seem . . . much to Agatha Christie Mallowan's chagrined annoyance.

After all, what on earth could be more innocent than a nursery rhyme? She enjoyed the irony of using a children's chant in an adult tale of murder—some time ago she'd done a short story called "Sing a Song of Six Pence," and was even now noodling with a plot for a Poirot to be called *Five Little Pigs*. That anyone might take offense at a play named after an old English counting rhyme—in which ten little boys, one by one, disappear—seemed utterly absurd to Agatha.

She had been forced to change the title to *Ten Little Indians* for publication of the source novel and production of the play in the United States, where the final word of her own title was considered offensive to the Negro race—so much so, that the movie the Americans were planning was to be christened with the last line of the rhyme-in-question: *And Then There Were None*. Apparently, dating all the way back to their Civil War, in America the term "nigger" referred exclusively, and in a derogatory fashion, to Negroes (whereas in England, of course, it might refer to any member of any darker-skinned race).

Surprisingly, according to her producer, there had even been complaints here at home. These related to the large influx of American Negro soldiers, who suffered prejudicial treatment from their own fellow soldiers, the white ones, that is.

Londoners like Agatha found this confusing and disturbing, and minor scandals had erupted all over town as restaurants catering to the well-moneyed American soldiers refused service not only to Negro soldiers but coloured Britons as well. Shockingly, Learie Constantine, the renowned West Indian cricketeer, had been turned away from the Imperial Hotel because American guests had threatened to cancel their reservations.

These Americans were strange ducks—fighting a war against Hitler and his Master Race and his concentration-camp hatred of the Jews, and yet displaying a deep-seated hateful bigotry both primitive and tasteless.

Of course, some considered Agatha herself tasteless, in her insistence that her nursery-rhyme title remain; her view: the rhyme was innocent and so was her use of it, free of the hatefulness the Americans read into mere words. She meant no offense and would not be responsible if offense was taken.

Still, Agatha had capitulated about her title where the American market was concerned; but this was England, and her title would stand (besides, the American "Indian" title seemed to refer to a stateside counting rhyme of banal simplicity . . . one little, two little, three little Indians . . . ugh!).

But these were strange times, indeed. That a play should be mounted in Blitz-torn London would have been unthinkable, just two years ago. At first there had been a ban on entertainment; soon, for purposes of morale, the ban was lifted. Younger actors could even seek dispensation from military service, providing they were not out of work for more than two weeks at a time. Few took advantage of this, however—such stars as Lawrence Olivier and Ralph Richardson had answered the call, and set a fine example.

Only at the height of the bombings did the theaters close, and the cinemas never did. And by the end of last year, twenty-four West End theaters were again flourishing. True, the fare tended to be light—revues, revivals, and comedies like the American imports *The Man Who Came to Dinner* and *Arsenic and Old Lace*, and Noel Coward's wonderful *Blithe Spirit*.

She hoped a murder thriller—one with darkly comic overtones—could find audiences willing to suspend their disbelief in these dark times.

And the moment did seem right for Agatha to get back in the theatrical swing. She adored the theater—going to it, and writing for it; she treasured the respect the playwright was given, and loved being around the larger-than-life characters who flocked to the bright lights of the West End.

Theater was a bug she had caught back in the early twenties, when her sister Madge's play, *The Claimant*, was produced in London, and Agatha had attended rehearsals with Madge, thoroughly enjoying this glimpse at the theatrical life. As her work at the hospital allowed, Agatha had attended rehearsals of this new play—she would not admit it to a living soul, but hearing her words spoken aloud, seeing her story brought to life, thrilled her in a way that quite outdistanced the printed page.

And she much preferred adapting her own work to the stage, rather than leaving it to someone else. The compromises that had been required to bring *The Murder of Roger Ackroyd* to the stage (as *Alibi* in 1928) troubled her even now—namely, the spinster village gossip who had been youthened into a love interest . . . for the elderly Poirot, no less!

And yet, for one who had loved attending plays since childhood—to this day she would seek out the scores of musicals she'd seen, to play the tunes on the piano— seeing her "baby" on the boards, even in bastardized form, had been thrilling. The next time, she had written the play herself, so when, about a year ago, Reginald Simpson—who had produced *Alibi*—inquired into theatrical rights to her nursery-rhyme novel, Agatha had straightened her spine and said, "If anyone is to dramatize it, I'll have a shot at it first."

The play had turned out remarkably well, particularly considering the difficulties of the original ending. In the novel, ten people from various walks of life—all guilty of (and unpunished for) a murder—are invited under false pretenses to an island mansion . . . where one by one, a vengeful murderer among them strikes them down.

She had come up with a new ending that she feared was a cheat, but which everyone assured her was ingenious; and in rehearsal the finale did seem to play very well indeed.

Of course, there was another reason Agatha had turned to writing a new play—a frankly monetary one. Because of wartime restrictions on paper, her publisher was printing only a limited number of copies of her new novels, and she was being encouraged to restrict her literary output somewhat, as well.

This came at a particularly bad moment, because her

American royalties were being held up, due to the war, while at the same time, the British government was insisting she pay taxes on those as yet unreceived American funds. Her attorneys were fighting for her—over what seemed clearly, even absurdly a taxation injustice—but at present the threat remained: her income was diminishing while her tax responsibilities soared.

Jumping back into the theatrical soup was a pleasant enough way to generate some earnings. During the Blitz period—at least when the bombs weren't dropping—the theater was a respite of escape for many Londoners like Agatha, whose letters to her husband, overseas in the Middle East, were filled with reports of new plays, even down to comparing her own opinions with extracts from critics.

And now the first night of her controversially titled new play was only a few days away. At the moment she was seated in the stalls of the St. James Theatre, rather near the front, with the director—Irene Helier—on one side of her, and Irene's husband, Bertram Morris, the producer, on the other.

A spiral notebook (containing the script and various other materials) open and in her lap, Irene was a strikingly beautiful woman of forty, with dark blue eyes and a pale perfect complexion, formerly an actress herself, whose minimal make-up, short dark hair, and mannish tan blouse and darker brown pants provided a military demeanor clearly designed to keep her femininity at bay while she took command of this little theatrical army.

Her husband, Bertram, was a short, bald, rather round man who had made a star of Irene twenty years ago and a director of her this year. A dapper dresser, Bertram was attired in a dark brown suit with yellow shirt and golden tie; his attire was always so handsome, Agatha felt, one could almost mistake *him* for handsome.

Almost.

After all, his features were those of a leading man, albeit condemned to that round face. He was a frog who had been kissed back into a prince, only to have the transformation stall, halfway.

The theater's lights were up, and the bare stage was well illuminated, as well. The naked shabbiness of the undressed stage made a marked contrast with the dignified elegance of the theater itself—dark wood paneling and rounded pillars and arched proscenium around which carved angels flew.

On the other hand, Agatha knew, theater was illusion, and under the seats of this elegant showcase could no doubt be found the hard-crusted corpses of abandoned chewing gum.

Speaking of which, the actress currently on stage, script in hand, was removing hers, delicately, a little embarrassed about it, as a stagehand scurried out to provide a napkin for the gum's disposal. The stagehand rushed off, like a member of the Unexploded Bomb detail looking for a bucket of water into which to drop an explosive device.

"So sorry," the actress said, in an alto that had a nice quality, to Agatha's ears. Chewing gum or not, the young woman possessed a voice with a dignified, even upper-class lilt; of course, she was an actress. Take Bertie, for example—he sounded as if he might have attended Oxford, whereas his father was a Whitechapel butcher, and the school the producer had graduated from was Hard Knocks.

The actress was not young—thirty-odd, Agatha should say—but she was quite attractive, a bright-eyed brunette with a heart-shaped face, cupie-doll red-rouged lips and a curvy shape that asserted itself despite a restrained wardrobe: dark gray suit jacket over off-white blouse, lighter gray skirt, brown "tanned" legs (*that liquid stockings stuff*, Agatha thought).

Standing next to her, making the five foot five woman look exceedingly small, was actor Francis L. Sullivan, who (like the young woman) had folded-open script in hand. The rather beefy actor stood a good six feet two, double-chinned and hooded-eyed, not unpleasant-looking, but no leading man.

Larry Sullivan had been the original Poirot in *Alibi* and had repeated the role in the recent *Peril at End House*. (*Why on earth*, Agatha wondered, *did producers insist on casting these ponderous overweight figures as her tiny Belgian detective? Charles Laughton's size in* Black Coffee *had been exceeded only by his overacting.*) Sullivan was not appearing in the current production—Poirot was not a character in this one—and had been called in as a dialogue coach at the last moment.

The female understudy—who would substitute for the crucial roles of Vera and Mrs. Brent—had vacated her duties last week, when she landed a better role in a revue. In normal times, this might have ended up with the understudy finding herself blacklisted in the West

End; but everyone knew the difficulties of assembling a qualified cast in wartime.

In particular, good actors were hard to come by—those men who preferred not to go into uniform were required to go out on one or two tours a year for ENSA (Entertainments National Service Associations). And pretty young actresses were much in demand for revues; among the many wartime shortages in London was an undersupply of chorus girls.

Irene's strong voice—a contralto—came from next to Agatha and echoed through the theater. *"Your name, please,"* she intoned, the voice of a female God.

Despite this, on the stage, the young woman seemed quite at ease. "Nita Ward," she said.

On the other side of Agatha, Bertie boomed: "Ah, yes, Miss Ward! So glad you could come."

"Thank you, Mr. Morris," Miss Ward said.

Bertie sat forward and spoke to his wife in a whisper. "Take a look at her resume, dear. She has impressive credits."

Irene glanced sharply at her husband. "Is that what you call them? . . . Did you invite this one?"

"Well . . ."

"Is this another of your discoveries, Bertram?"

"Darling . . . she's qualified. Please do look at her vita."

Another sharp look from Irene. "Why should I? . . . You seem to have examined Nita's . . . *vita*, already."

Agatha felt that she had suddenly become the net in a tennis match. A grudge match, at that.

A notion, the cattiness of which was worthy of Jane Marple herself, flashed through Agatha's mind: Perhaps Irene was doomed to such jealousies, since she better than anyone knew how an actress could get ahead in the theatrical world, particularly with this producer . . . .

"You can be impossible, sometimes," Bertie said, and rose, and shuffled out of the aisle to take a seat elsewhere, nearer to the stage . . . and to his latest discovery?

Irene, coldly professional, called out, "If you would take it from Act Three, Scene Two. . . . Larry, you'll read both Blore and Lombard."

The young woman was nothing special, but she had a lively quality and did not trip over the words. She was the seventh woman they'd heard read for the understudy part this afternoon, and by some distance the best.

"Her age is about right," Agatha ventured in a whisper to Irene.

"She's not bad," Irene admitted. "She's a bit short."

"Oh, I think that's just Larry. He's a towering beast, our Larry."

Irene laughed a little. "Yes . . . he wouldn't have been bad as the judge."

"You have a splendid judge. Larry can be a bit . . ."

"Bombastic," Irene said.

"Indeed. . . . Lovely man, though."

"Thank you!" Irene called out to the scene. "If you'll hold up, just a moment, please. . . ." The director looked behind her. "Janet!"

Janet Cummins, an attractive brunette in dark-rimmed glasses, rose from her aisle seat a few rows back and came down to meet Irene. Janet was Bertie's secretary, but that understated her role: she was a trusted assistant to both Irene and Bertie.

Odd, Agatha observed, that Irene had no jealousy over Janet, who was a fetching, busty, blue-eyed woman in her later twenties, business-like in a navy suit with white blouse.

"Yes, Miss Helier?" Janet asked, dutifully half-kneeling in the aisle, clipboard in hand.

"How many more?"

"We only have three more to see."

Irene was studying the stage where a friendly Miss Ward and a smiling Larry were conversing softly, pleasantly. "She really isn't terrible. . . . I'm going to read her some more."

Janet nodded, and then looked over at Agatha and whispered across Irene, "Could I have a word, Mrs. Mallowan?"

Agatha said, "Certainly, my dear."

Faintly irritated, Irene said to the assistant, "Come around and do it, then."

Janet crossed the row of seats behind them and entered from the aisle, sidling over, and was about to take the seat Bertie had vacated when Agatha rose and met her halfway, to put a few seats between them and Irene.

They sat.

Janet's eyes were tight behind the lenses. "Mrs. Mallowan, I hate to bother you. . . . I know how you feel about having a fuss made. . . ."

"Go on, my dear."

Janet seemed hesitant, even nervous, and was searching for words.

Gently Agatha prodded, "What is it, dear? I don't bite."

Janet's smile was embarrassed. "You've heard me mention Gordon . . ."

"Gordon?"

"My husband."

"Ah! The RAF pilot. Your brave young hero!"

"Well . . . I think he will be a hero, one day soon. He's learning to fly Spitfires, right now. . . . Anyway, he's such an enormous fan of yours. He's simply reading your books day and night, just devouring them, and, well, I wondered if you would mind saying hello to him. For me."

"Why, not at all! Shall we send him a signed book? Where is he stationed, dear?"

"Right here in London. Or that is, out at St. John's Wood."

"Oh, how lovely for you to have your man in the military so close by. Are you able to live together?"

"No, unfortunately. He's billeted near the station. But we see each other frequently."

Agatha gestured with open palms. "Well, why don't you invite him down to the theater, some afternoon, if he can get away from his duties? Or perhaps he could come to our opening night, on Friday."

Janet's embarrassed smile curdled into mortification. "Actually, I took the liberty . . . I talked to your friend. . . . Oh my."

"Please, Janet. You're making me out to be an absolute ogre. What is it?"

"Well . . . he's here now. Gordon's here."

Janet swiveled in her seat and indicated the back of the theater.

There, just inside the lobby, semi-silhouetted by mote-flecked sunlight, stood a young man in RAF blues, cap in both hands figleafed before him, a broad-shouldered sturdy five-nine or ten, a boyishly handsome specimen of Britain's military who might have stepped right off a recruiting poster.

Agatha touched Janet's hand. "By all means, dear, let's go back and say hello. I'd be honored to have you introduce me."

They moved to the rear of the theater, even as the audition continued, Miss Ward's voice resounding pleasantly through the stalls as she ably traded lines with Larry Sullivan. She was gaining confidence as the audition went on.

Gordon Cummins shifted on his feet, twisting his cap in his hands in anticipation as Agatha and Mrs. Cummins approached. His boyish good looks only improved on closer inspection—blondish brown hair, a fair complexion, wide-set eyes of a striking clear blue-green, like a country brook on a perfect afternoon. His nose was straight and well-formed, his mouth almost feminine in its poised-for-a-kiss sensuality.

Archie, Agatha thought, eyes widening, the sight of the young man hitting like a physical blow, the image of her first husband jumping into her mind in his own RAF uniform, of the last war. *I haven't seen such a handsome young man in uniform since Archie was my . . .*

"Mrs. Christie, this is such an honor," the young man blurted.

"Gordon," Janet whispered, scoldingly. "It's Mrs. Mallowan. I explained that . . ."

"It's all right, dear," Agatha said. "That's still my name, my professional name." She glanced toward the stage where the audition remained under way. "Shall we step into the lobby?"

They did.

The young man had a soft voice, a second tenor, and his manners were impeccable; Agatha noticed he wore a Leading Aircraftsman badge, the white badge (or "flash") of an Officer Trainee on the hat in his hands.

He was quite charming, really, in a naive way. For several minutes he raved on and on about her books, specifically the Poirot novels, and Agatha allowed herself to bask in the adulation. It was as if Archie were standing there praising her work, adoringly interested in her . . . which in the reality of their marriage had never occurred.

Finally she said, "You're very kind, Mr. Cummins. Tell me something about yourself."

"Not much to tell, really," he said, with a fleeting grin. "My father was a schoolmaster of sorts."

"That's sounds . . . educational."

Janet put in, "I'm afraid more so than you know, Mrs. Mallowan. Gordon's father was rather more a warden than a schoolmaster, I would say—the school was for delinquent boys and girls."

"Oh," Agatha said, and frowned sympathetically. "I

hope that wasn't terribly unpleasant for you. Was your father strict, then?"

"By most standards, yes," the boy said. "But it was good for me. Prepared me for the life I'm leading now."

Janet, rather proudly, said, "Gordon has something else in common with you, Mrs. Mallowan."

"Really? What is that, dear?"

"He's a chemist."

"Is that right, Mr. Cummins? You do know I work in a pharmacy."

"I do know," he said, "that you know your poisons."

They all laughed. A little.

Shyly, the cadet said, "I can't say my tour of duty as a chemist is anything to boast about—I trained in a Northampton technical school and worked here in London, as a research chemist."

"That's when we met," Janet explained. "I was already working for Mr. Morris."

Agatha bestowed on them a smile, one each; then to the young RAF cadet, she asked, "You enjoy the air force?"

"Very much! I'll be flying a Spitfire soon."

Janet said, "One of his senior officers—a Schneider Trophy pilot—has personally endorsed Gordon for his commission."

"How thrilling," Agatha said. "Do you think you can get a pass to join us on opening night?"

"That would be wonderful. I do so love the book!"

Her smile was apologetic. "Well, the play turns out a

little differently. . . . Why don't you come in and watch these auditions? We're finding an understudy for our leading lady."

Cummins sat toward the back as Agatha returned to Irene's side, while Janet headed to the stage and the wings, to direct traffic on the auditions. The pert Miss Ward was asked to stay around for a possible callback, and the other actresses read with Larry, none of them terribly good.

A thin blonde actress (who was forty-five if she was a day) was reading when Stephen Glanville strode down the aisle and, with his usual confidence, slid in and over and plopped down next to Agatha.

For an archaeologist, Glanville had personality to spare. He was tall, handsome, mustached, cleft-chinned, forty-two years of age, in a rumpled brown tweed suit with reddish brown bow tie that identified him as the professor he was; he was also the most despicable rake. Notwithstanding, he was Agatha's husband's best friend and sometime cohort in Egyptology, and—despite the man's faults—Agatha loved him dearly.

Glanville had taken a position in the RAF—strictly bureaucratic, at Whitehall—and had in fact engineered Max's commission. This had been an enormous favor to Max, whose heritage was against him, ridiculously enough; though born in England, and giving off an Oxbridge air, Max had nary a spot of English blood—French mother, Austrian father.

So it indeed was Stephen who'd wrangled Max that posting, as RAF Adviser on Arab Affairs to the British Military Government in Tripolitania, North Africa.

Agatha tried not to resent that Max was surrounded by the great sites of antiquity that were his passion, in a bungalow by the sea, with a warm climate and a diet of fresh fish and vegetables. Meanwhile she existed in cold, precarious London on bangers and mash.

Before Max's posting, Stephen had also helped Agatha and her husband find suitable lodging in London, in the same Lawn Road Flats where Glanville himself lived. Stephen's family, his wife and children, had long since been hastened off to Canada, for safety's sake; and in the meantime, Stephen Glanville was having one romantic affair after another.

Stephen did not bother hiding the fact from Agatha, who had become his sole confidant in Max's absence. He claimed these "flings" meant nothing to him, and were merely to console and comfort him in his family's absence.

They had spent many evenings alone together; Agatha often cooked for Glanville. She found the Egyptologist quite good-looking and she remained relieved—and vaguely insulted—that he had never made a play for her.

"I'm afraid I'm going to have to take the blame," Stephen whispered.

"That's because you're so frequently guilty," Agatha whispered back. She detected a frown from Irene, and motioned to Glanville to move a few seats over, so as not to disturb the director. Then: "Blame for what?"

"I'm afraid the presence of that fresh-faced fan from St. Wood's Station is my fault . . . or at least, partly mine."

Agatha glanced back at the handsome cadet, whose eyes were on the stage and the latest actress to trample on her words.

"Oh, he's quite charming," Agatha said. "Janet's a very lucky girl."

"Janet could do better than that cabbage," Stephen said. "But never mind."

Agatha turned and looked at her handsome friend. "You arranged for that cadet to have the afternoon off, didn't you, Stephen?"

He was a higher-up in the Air Ministry, after all.

He grinned. "Guilty as charged. . . . Janet told me the kid was a huge fan of yours. I warned her that you didn't like being fussed over. But Janet pleaded."

"Please tell me you don't have your sights on—"

"No! No. We're just pals, Janet and I. But I don't mind doing a favor for a pretty lady. One never knows with whom one might wind up stranded on a desert island."

Agatha shook her head. "Stephen, no one combines cynicism and romanticism quite so effectively as you. A unique gift, you have there."

"Thank you, my dear. That is . . . 'darling.' We are at the the-ah-tah, you know."

She again glanced at the cadet, entranced in the theatrical experience. "Well, I don't mind meeting a loyal reader. . . . and, anyway, I don't have 'fans,' Stephen, I have readers . . . customers. I just don't care for mobs of them. One on one, they can be quite delightful."

"He is a good-looking bloke, I'll give you that."

"He's young enough to be my son."

"Ah, but he isn't. Your son, I mean. So incest isn't really an issue, is it?"

She looked sideways at him. "You're a terrible man, Stephen. A true villain."

"Then why do you love me?"

She shrugged. "There's no explaining it."

"So when do we begin?"

His voice had naughtiness in it—as if he were finally referring to an affair.

"Begin what?"

"Our book! Our Egyptian mystery."

"I've told you before, Stephen—I never collaborate."

"I don't want to collaborate. I merely want to advise. What a wonderful surprise for Max to return and find you've set your latest thriller in ancient Egypt."

They'd had this conversation endlessly, since Max departed.

And it ended as it always did: "We shall see, Stephen."

Then she told Stephen about her research project with Sir Bernard Spilsbury.

"That sounds dangerous," Stephen said skeptically.

"Don't be silly. I may be going to crime scenes, is all—the danger's long over, by the time the pathologist arrives."

"Still . . . I don't like it. I doubt Max would like it, either."

"He would have the same reaction as you, dear Stephen: a knee jerk of chauvinism; and then I would point out that Sir Bernard's research is not unlike his own . . . digging into the past. And that my work, at least as I see it right now, requires a research effort of my own. And I would have Max's blessing."

His dark eyes were tight beneath the dark eyebrows. "I don't know, Agatha. Do please take care."

"Who's to say anything will come of it? This 'Ripper' may never strike again; or the two murders may not really be connected."

Stephen shifted uncomfortably in the hard seat. "But if a new Jack the Ripper *is* stalking London, using the blackout as his fog . . . that's inherently dangerous. You must reconsider."

"I tell you what, Stephen. Stay away from the likes of Janet Cummins, and I'll consider . . . reconsidering."

"You're a cruel woman, Mrs. Mallowan."

"*Mrs. Mallowan!*" The seeming echo was Irene calling over to her. "Agatha . . . a moment, please?"

Agatha gave Stephen a scolding look, said, "Behave yourself while I'm gone," and returned to the seat next to the director.

"I hate to interrupt your social hour," Irene said, teasing good humor mixed in with the bitchiness. "But have you had the opportunity to pay any attention to these auditions?"

"I have indeed."

"I'm on the fence. There are three I'm considering."

"No, you're not, Irene. You know very well the Ward girl is the best. The others are quite wretched. Miss Ward is the most attractive, and she speaks my lines well . . . or at any rate, well enough."

Irene sighed. "I hate to give a part to one of Bertie's 'discoveries.' "

Agatha touched the director's arm. "Bertie loves only you, Irene. Just as you love only the theater. Cast the best girl—which is to say, Miss Ward."

The next sigh was colossal. "Well . . . I'll read her again, at least."

Nita Ward returned and by this time she and Larry Sullivan were old pals, laughing, touching each other. Agatha had never considered Larry to have a philandering bone in his body; but a fetching creature like Nita Ward, even if she had been around the block a few times, could probably locate that bone quite easily.

"The same two scenes, please," Irene called. "Larry, again, please read both parts."

And the theater filled itself with Agatha Christie's lines, and Mrs. Mallowan was quite enchanted . . .

. . . at least until she began to wonder if her ten little whimsical murders . . . her murders for fun . . . had a place in a world at war, and a city "stalked" (as Stephen had aptly if archly put it) by a Ripper.

February 10, 1942

The West End seemed rife with men in uniform these days, but not every bloke in khaki got respect, much less the perks of wartime enjoyed by so many. Still, Inspector First Class did sound impressive, didn't it?

And would have been, were Jack Rawlins a police officer, say, and not a reader of shilling-in-the-slot electrical meters for the light company.

At thirty-six, an eighteen-year veteran among electrical "inspectors," Rawlins had seen every bleeding thing in this business, from opulence to squalor, big fat women just stepped from the tub, lovely lithe ladies alighting from the shower (latter such instances were pressed in Rawlins's mental memory book like flowers, while the former he strove to forget). Barking dogs, untended babies, passed-out drunks—what hadn't he stumbled across in his duties for God, country and paycheck?

And in spite of the lack of respect for his branch of the service, Rawlins experienced his share of hazardous duty on these Blitz-torn streets, stepping over fire hoses, skirting craters, veering to avoid UXBs. When a bomb disrupted normal electrical services, was it a soldier or sailor who charged into the breech? Hell no! It was the fearless likes of Jack Rawlins. . . .

You might think working the Soho district would be glamorous or at least interesting. But the "foreign" quarter of the West End—enclosed by Wardour Street, Shaftesbury Avenue, Charing Cross Road and Oxford Street—was as dull by day as it was provocative by night. Right about now, just before eight-thirty in the morning, the snow-flecked sidewalks were largely empty, the streetwalkers of Soho tucked in their wee beds, doing nothing at all spectacular, and the array of unique nightclubs and exotic restaurants wouldn't be open for business till much later in the day.

In fact, Rawlins made a point of doing the flats above first, as it was difficult finding anyone in the clubs and restaurants till late morning, when they were either open for lunch or cleaning up for the coming night (and didn't those "unique" nightclubs and "exotic" restaurants look disappointedly drab and dirty by the light of day).

The shops and businesses and such weren't open yet, either, like this optician's at 153 Wardour Street, which was next on his route. Rawlins headed up the narrow unlighted flight of stairs to a small landing and a quartet of doors to a trio of flats and a shared bathroom; a yellow hanging bulb threw a pool of light for him to stand in, as if he were on stage. He'd encountered the woman who lived alone there, now and then—a pleasant, pleasantly plumpish and oh so pretty prostitute, name of Evelyn Oatley.

Rawlins was a happily married man, however, and considered himself immune to Miss Oatley's charms. Besides, what beauty offered to swap services with a meter reader to save a shilling? Not that he would have looked away, should he stumble onto the fetching fallen flower alighting from her bath. . . .

When he knocked, the door creaked open a few inches; he had not realized it was ajar.

"Miss Oatley!" he called. "Here to read your meter, miss!"

No answer.

Shrugging to himself, Rawlins stepped inside.

The small one-room apartment was quite dark, the curtains still drawn. He tried the light switch, but the slot meter's money had run out and the light did not turn on; seemed he'd come 'round none too soon.

With no one home, Rawlins probably should have backed out of the flat and gone about his business. But the nape of his neck was prickling—it was not like Miss Oatley to allow her electricity to run out like that. She kept a small neat flat and was pretty enough to make her illicit way in the world, easily.

Rawlins took the small electric torch from his tool belt and switched it on, just to check things out a bit . . .

. . . and the shaft of light fell immediately upon Miss Oatley.

She lay sprawled on her back on her divan bed, head back and hanging over, clad only in a thin sheer nightgown, which was open to reveal her in nakedness, which might have been titillating to a red-blooded man like Rawlins.

But it was not, though this sight would be pressed, involuntarily, into his mental memory book; and the electrician immediately realized he had not seen every bleeding thing, after all. . . .

Because the plumply pretty prostitute was quite dead, her throat slashed, the blood having run down to gather and coagulate into a terrible black pool.

Heart in his throat, Jack Rawlins scurried out of the flat and down the steps onto the street, where he quickly found a bobby and reported what he'd discovered . . .

. . . not feeling much at all like one man in uniform talking to another.

FOUR

Dressed for Murder

It seemed to Agatha that Hampstead was quite the most rustic and sweetly antiquated of the suburban districts of Central London, blessedly free from major Blitz damage, with narrow lanes leading to sequestered spots so sheltered from the tumult of town that one could close one's eyes halfway and imagine being in a country village.

Built in a haphazardly irregular fashion on the hill sloping up to the Heath, Hampstead would have been perhaps the most nightmarish place in the city for her symmetry-obsessed detective, Hercule Poirot. But spinster Jane Marple would have loved it—wide High Street with its old brick houses adapted to shops and businesses, an inviting maze of courtyards and passageways and byways, streets lined with elms shading country-style cottages with perfectly manicured front lawns.

Even the modern blocks of two-story brick Bauhaus flats somehow suited the old-world atmosphere. Agatha's apartment at 22 Lawn Road was like a small gabled house, and had been perfect and cozy when she and Max had shared it. Since her husband's posting overseas, the place felt to Agatha large and cold, but that was half psychology and half the winter weather.

The two-floor apartment that was the Mallowan portion of the connected Bauhaus flats had come furnished—just as well, as after the bombing at Sheffield Terrace, all their furniture had been stored in the new Winterbrook squash court in Wallingford. These accommodations pleased her—the neighbors were friendly but unobtrusive (nary a question about "Agatha Christie" since she'd moved in)—and the building included a small unpretentious restaurant where she took many of her meals. She loved to cook, but when provisions were so hard to come by, a decent close-at-hand restaurant like this one was a godsend.

In the summer the Lawn Road Flats were most pleasant, with a garden ideal for little picnics; she was particularly taken with the bank of trees and shrubs behind the building, and in the spring, a big white cherry tree that rose to a pyramidal point presented itself, in all its blooming glory, just outside her second-floor bedroom window, encouraging her to rise with a smile even in wartime.

The only furniture she'd imported were her basic office accouterments: large firm table and typewriter and hard upright chair for writing, and her comfy old easy chair for thinking. She set herself up in the library-style study—whose empty shelves stared accusingly at her until, some months later, she'd half-filled them with reference works, mostly medical and chemistry tomes—where (as was her habit) she removed the phone.

Oh, and one other thing: a spinet piano. She could not exist without a piano; life would not have been worth living. This she kept in the library as well, because intermissions of music between bouts of writing and thinking she found frankly therapeutic.

Her only company—outside of Stephen Glanville popping in twice or thrice a week, from a few doors down—was the Sealyham terrier, James. He was a playful pup, beautifully housebroken (James, not Stephen), and excellent company when she walked to Hampstead Heath, four-hundred-and-twenty acres of delightful grassy common, perfect for picnics and walks among the wooded groves and open spaces. What heaven it was to sit nibbling an apple, gazing out at rippling glassy lakes where young lovers rowed.

But it was winter now, with snow on the common, and that left only work—work at the hospital by day (and occasional evenings), work by night in the library on her novels and stories and plays. Few would have guessed that for Agatha writing was a chore, as tedious as doing the dishes, as hard as chopping wood . . . harder—or that she would much rather have spent her time cooking or gardening or going on outings with (the absent) Max.

Or better still, being out on a dig with Max, lovely sun beating down, pearls of well-earned perspiration gliding decoratively over her cheeks, as she assisted the man she loved in his truly important efforts (as opposed to the trivialities of her own "career").

And yet still, somehow, if not by nature then through the accumulation of time and effort, she had become a writer; and writing never left her. Even now, as she sat in the cheery, informal little Lawn Road Flats restaurant—Tuesday morning, a respectable-looking matron (a matron already! what a horror!) in sensible brown tweed and a cream silk blouse, remindful of a femininity she had not (yet) abandoned—she noodled on the plotting and characters of the next Poirot in a small black spiral notebook . . .

. . . not unlike the notebooks in which Sir Bernard Spilsbury recorded the clues relating to his very real crimes.

And that gave her a shudder of revulsive self-recognition, a shameful shiver of senselessness. Like Max, Sir Bernard did important work. His notebook entries dealt with real mysteries, not fanciful ones. Whatever useful purpose in this war-torn world might her work serve?

The only response she could come up with was, perhaps, a self-serving rationalization; recalling that RAF cadet she'd met yesterday, that brave lad whose life would soon be on the line for his country, Agatha knew that her silly little novels gave that hero-to-be solace, distracted him briefly from the problems of his real, very unpleasant world.

She wondered if that were justification enough.

Sipping her coffee (that she preferred the brew to

tea seemed somehow unpatriotic), Agatha had another mental flash, suddenly remembering a dream she'd had last night. Usually her dreams left her within seconds of rising; other times she could vividly recall them long enough for her to record them in one of her notebooks . . . you never knew what mental trifle might prove useful in the writing game.

The reason this dream had come back to her in so whole a state (and she had no notion whatever what subconscious nudge had brought it suddenly to the surface) was simple enough: this was a recurring dream, a dream she'd had (variously revised) many, many times. . . .

The nightmare dated to childhood and centered upon a figure she had come to term "the Gunman," a handsome French soldier with a powdered wig, three-cornered hat and a musket, his eyes a haunting, piercing light blue. Oddly, the figure in her nocturnal fantasies had never done anything threatening, much less shoot the weapon at her: it was his very presence, specifically his incongruous presence, that frightened her.

This dream figure of potential violence initially had turned up in a children's party, where he would enter and ask to join the game. Later versions found him sitting at a tea table with an otherwise benign group of Agatha's friends and relations; sometimes, in an eyeblink, her mother or sister or a chum would be replaced by the blue-eyed Gunman; other times she would be walking along the beach with a friend and then, suddenly, he and his weapon would be beside her, instead.

Agatha felt strongly that there was no simplistically Freudian aspect to the dream—she had been very young when the Gunman dreams first began; and, anyway, she understood psychology well enough to know that if the figure had shot her or even threatened to shoot her, a sexual connotation might be drawn.

But Sigmund himself had said it, hadn't he? Sometimes a banana simply was a banana.

Nor did she recall any storybook that she might have read as a child (or had read to her), whose vivid illustration of a soldier might have planted this seed of fright.

The most disturbing of the dreams had been during her marriage to Archie. Even before their relationship had begun to deteriorate, she would dream of blue-eyed Archie—in his uniform of the Great War—metamorphosing into the blue-eyed Gunman. Chilling how little difference there was between the fantasy figure and the real Archie, how small a metamorphosis was required.

Odd, wasn't it? Even as a child she'd had an instinct that people were not always who or what they seemed, that even a friend or family member might become someone, something, sinister. Perhaps this was why she had been drawn to writing mysteries in which violence and menace lay beneath the humdrum surface of everyday living.

"I hate to interrupt this reverie," a familiar voice said.

She looked up at her friend and neighbor, Stephen Glanville, a typically devilish grin on that Ronald Colmanesque, dimple-chinned face. Both dashing and professorial in a light gray tweed suit with dark gray bow tie, Stephen had some folded newspapers tucked under one arm, and was leaning on the chair opposite her at the small table.

"Please join me, Stephen."

He did. "You looked perfectly glazed over, when I came in. I trust you're lost in thought, devising fiendish plot twists for our Egyptian mystery."

Archaeologists were, by nature, a persistent lot.

"Actually, I'm fiddling with the new Poirot idea."

"I thought you despised the little bastard—if you'll pardon my French. Or in this case, Belgian."

"Stephen—please. Whatever I may think of the little monster, he is popular with my readers, and their opinions count more than mine. . . . Shouldn't you be at Whitehall?"

He glanced at his watch. "I'm due at the ministry in half an hour. I have time for a cup and a quick hello."

A waitress brought Stephen tea, and he said to Agatha, "I'm glad I found you here."

"It's nice to be appreciated. . . . Why?"

"Then I trust you haven't seen the press?" He folded open the newspapers, and a particularly vile tabloid was on top: the front page asked, LONDON PLAGUED BY NEW RIPPER?

"I don't read *The News of the World*," Agatha said, with prim disgust.

"Someone at the Yard must be on the payroll. Several someones, judging by the various stories." The other papers had also picked up on the Maple Church and Evelyn Hamilton murders, Stephen showed her, though none as blatantly as the tabloid.

"Typically irresponsible," Agatha said. "Two murdered women does not a 'new' Ripper make."

"No, but some 'confidential source' has shared the fears of Inspector Greeno and your friend Sir Bernard that these killings may mean a blackout Ripper is among us. Sells papers."

"And creates panic. Disgraceful."

"I know how you feel about the newspapers, Agatha . . ."

She said nothing.

She trusted Stephen knew not to enter forbidden territory. Even after all these years, the discomfort, the embarrassment of a certain newspaper campaign remained a palpable presence in her psyche. When she had fled her problems with Archie and his philandering, seeking sanctuary at a health resort, the press had treated her "disappearance" as major news, and then, when she had turned up alive and well (considering), had accused her of staging a publicity stunt.

From that time on, she felt a revulsion toward the press, a dislike for journalists and their undue, tasteless attention. She knew first-hand how a fox felt—hunted, the earth dug up around her, hounds snapping at her every step.

"You are the rare public figure, Agatha, who deplores notoriety. Most authors seek publicity."

"The work is the work, Stephen. My life is my life. And my own."

"I know. I hope I have not overstepped. . . ."

"Not yet."

He sighed. Sipped his tea. Sat back in the hard chair.

Folded his arms. Said, "That's why I have sought you out, to ask you one last time to reconsider the foolishness of involving yourself with Spilsbury and these Ripper crimes."

"The *press* has designated them Ripper crimes. I do not necessarily think—"

He raised a hand, stopping her in mid-sentence. "I bring these papers 'round only to let you know what you may be in for. If the press detects your presence, even on the fringes of this matter, you may be in for an unpleasantness for which you are wholly unprepared."

She frowned in thought. "Stephen . . . I admit to you that this had not occurred to me. Thank you for pointing it out."

He leaned forward, touched her hand. "Then you have reconsidered. You'll stay well out of this."

"No. But I will take precautions to avoid journalists in the matter."

His face fell. "Agatha . . . tell me truthfully. Does Max ever win an argument with you?"

"We don't argue. We discuss."

"And do you always prevail?"

"Certainly not. But then Max is my husband . . . you're merely my friend."

He chuckled. "With precious little influence, obviously. . . . Oh, I must run."

He came around, kissed her cheek, and was gone.

Back in the flat, in the library, Agatha sat in her easy chair, making notes on the Poirot; but Stephen's concerns about the press, his warning, lingered.

The telephone rang out in the hall, and she allowed

herself to be interrupted; she wasn't getting much work done, anyway. The phone was on a stand just around the foot of the stairs. The caller proved to be Sir Bernard.

"I am taking you at your word," he said.

"I would expect nothing else."

"Well, our murderer has struck again. I've been called to the scene—over Soho way, not far from Piccadilly. Shall I come 'round and pick you up?"

"Are you at the hospital?"

"Actually I'm at my flat."

Sir Bernard lived with his sister Constance on nearby Frognal Street; he and Agatha were practically neighbors.

"I could pick you up," he was saying, "in a matter of minutes."

"Please do."

"Mrs. Mallowan . . . Agatha. I'm told it's unpleasant."

"It's a murder, isn't it?"

"Indeed," he said, with an air of understanding.

And they said good-byes and hung up.

Agatha had already assembled a crime-scene wardrobe. She had given it considerable thought, actually. The weather was brisk if not brutally cold, but she could hardly wear a fur coat to a murder—this was not, after all, a first night at the theater.

Nor did she wish to present either an overly feminine or schoolteacher matronly appearance. She chose a wardrobe that seemed to her suitably appropriate for detective work, and only hoped she had not inadvertently stooped to melodramatically theatrical effects.

The suit was a mannish pastel beige affair, jacket

with cardigan neckline and patch pockets, skirt pleated front and back. To the Glen Plaid tones-of-brown woolen topcoat—boyish-looking with its flap pockets and raised welt seams on the sleeves and in back—she added a mannish wide-brimmed light brown felt hat with darker brown band.

The latter was enough like a man's fedora to make her wonder if she might not be pushing her detective credentials; but it was the current style. . . .

Sir Bernard, however, wore no topcoat at all. In his crisp black suit with his characteristic red carnation in its buttonhole, he might have been the best-tailored undertaker in town. He seemed oblivious to (or perhaps contemptuous of) the chill weather.

Agatha, who loved to drive and had a reckless streak herself, found the experience of being Sir Bernard's passenger in his Armstrong-Siddeley sedan a surprising if not wholly pleasant one. For an individual who appeared the soul of moderation—she had seen no signs that he either smoked or drank—the pathologist took liberties with traffic lights and one-way streets that would have inspired fines and perhaps jail time for any mere citizen.

That the streets were so relatively barren of vehicles made the journey only frightening and not terrifying.

She attempted to slow his passage with conversation, but this had no apparent effect, and after one exchange on one subject, Agatha lapsed to silence.

That one exchange, however, was significant.

"Bernard," she said, "I do have a concern."

"What is that, Agatha?" he asked, careening around a corner down the wrong way of a one-way street, pedestrian eyes only slightly wider than if their bearers had just heard an air raid siren's banshee cry.

"These murders," she said, hanging on to a door strap, "have already attracted the attention of the gutter press."

"Unfortunately, yes. And not just the tabloids, I'm afraid. Deplorable that this 'Ripper' connection has been made. Creates a difficult atmosphere in which to work."

"That's my concern, as well. I don't know if you're aware that I have a distinct aversion for publicity. . . ."

"I was not, but I'm relieved to hear it."

He slowed, barely, before running a STOP signal.

"Relieved?"

"Yes. I take you at your word that your interest in this case is scientific—background research. If the notion here was to attract the press to a 'collaboration' between the foremost forensics man and the world's greatest mystery writer . . . well. I could not be party to that."

"I abhor the press."

"As do I," he said, almost spinning the steering wheel, narrowly missing a bicyclist. "The newspapers have published an unending parade of lies and legends about me, exaggerating my career. I'm afraid I've developed an almost morbid aversion to publicity."

Had they not been flying down a West End street like an ambulance, this confirmation would have warmed the cockles of Agatha's heart.

"I have," Sir Bernard continued, "made it clear that my participation as pathologist on call to Scotland Yard is contingent upon one condition: that I be protected from the press. . . . That shielding, my dear, will be extended to you."

"Wonderful! Bernard . . ."

"Yes, Agatha?"

"Do you by any chance have a siren?"

"No." He glanced at her, the soul of placid gravity. "This is not an official police vehicle. . . . Why do you ask?"

"Nothing. Merely a point of research."

Detective Chief Inspector Edward Greeno was waiting for them on Wardour Street, standing before a gigantic Dali-esque eye painted upon the window of an optician's shop. The inspector, puffing on a pool-cue of a cigar, looked every inch the detective of film and fiction—a broad-shouldered bulldog in a snapbrim fedora and extravagantly lapelled trench coat.

Upon seeing Sir Bernard and Agatha approaching, the inspector dropped his cigar—though it was only half-smoked—and quickly ground it out with his heel on the pavement. Then he met them halfway, introducing himself, bowing to Agatha, who presented him a hand to shake, man-to-man fashion; he accepted her hand, grinning at her, his expression rather foolish.

"Excuse me for smiling under such conditions," the inspector said, "but I have to admit, Mrs. Christie, that I am a big reader of yours."

Sir Bernard—standing with an almost absurdly oversize black Gladstone bag in hand, looking like an impatient doctor making a house call (which was the case, actually)—crisply corrected Inspector Greeno.

"That's her writing name, Inspector. This is Mrs. Mallowan. Her husband is the noted archaeologist."

The inspector nodded a curt apology, saying, "Mrs. Mallowan. . . . A lot of the boys read your books. We feel as though we could use that little Belgian of yours, from time to time."

"Inspector," she said, "I am pleased and relieved by your attitude. I was afraid I would be considered a sort of fifth wheel. I can only assure you I will touch nothing and stay well out of everyone's way."

"Just the mouse in the corner, eh? You may spend a good deal of time out on the landing, I'm afraid, as it's a small flat."

"I will do as I'm told, Inspector."

Another grin creased the bulldog face. "Well, Sir Bernard vouches for you, and the Home Office has given out instructions to treat you royally . . . which for a fan like me will be a pleasure."

Sir Bernard said, "One small point, Inspector—Mrs. Mallowan has the same aversion to publicity that I do."

"I'm ahead of you, Doctor. I'll tell you I was mad as hell . . . excuse me, Mrs. Mallowan . . . about this press leak. Last thing we needed was panic on the West End, over a so-called 'Ripper' . . . and now, I'm afraid, we indeed have one."

Agatha frowned. "One what, Inspector?"

"A ripper. The doctor has described the other two murders to you, in some detail, I understand."

"He has."

"Well, this time we have a bona fide ripper-style sexual mutilation." Gently, tentatively, Inspector Greeno touched the sleeve of her Glen Plaid. "And I did want to warn you, Mrs. Christie . . . Mrs. Mallowan. This is pure savagery, it is. You may wish to spare yourself the—"

"Inspector, I work with Sir Bernard at University College Hospital. My background is that of a nurse dealing with the combat wounded. Need I say more about my lack of squeamishness?"

"Not at all, Mrs. Mallowan."

"May I take notes?"

"You may." He gestured with a thick finger to the flat above the optician's. "Initially we'll stay out on the landing. I've had some photographs taken, but my procedure is always to preserve the crime scene as much as possible, until Sir Bernard arrives. . . . Shall we go on up?"

Inspector Greeno led the way, his voice echoing up the dim narrow stairwell. "Her name was Evelyn Oatley. Meter-reader found her. Our assumption is that she's one of the working girls here in Soho."

By this, Agatha knew, the inspector meant the woman had been a prostitute.

A uniformed police officer waited on the landing. He said to Greeno, "I'll just get out of your way, Governor," and headed down the stairs to stand watch on the street, thus making room in the small space for the inspector and Agatha. In the meantime, Sir Bernard went on through the open door into the flat, where the electric lights were on.

"The only thing I touched, Doctor," the inspector said to the pathologist's back, "was the electrical meter. Hope putting a shilling in the slot won't do any harm."

Sir Bernard said nothing. He set his big Gladstone bag down with a slight clank. At first he was blocking the body, which lay sprawled on a divan-style bed in the single-room flat. Carefully stepping over a vast pool of dried blood, the pathologist walked around the body, studying it, at times leaning almost close enough to kiss the dead woman's naked flesh.

Intermittently, Agatha's view of the corpse improved until she had seen it all too well.

The victim was thirty-odd, curvaceous and quite attractive in an apple-cheeked cupie-doll manner. Her throat had been cut—a wide, thin gash, like a terrible thin-lipped smile below her chin; and the lower part of the woman's body, near her sexual organs, had been viciously slashed.

"When we interviewed the electrician," the inspector said to Agatha, his voice soft and conversational, "he seemed quite sure Miss Oatley was a prostitute."

"Do you think he was a client?"

The inspector's quick look showed surprise at this frankness on Agatha's part. "I asked him that. He said no, even when I assured him no charges would be proffered and it would be kept strictly confidential."

"Had he ever spoken to the girl? Just a chat when he dropped around to read the meter?"

"Yes. He said Miss Oatley was a nice kid, a bubbly sort, not at all down about her lot in life. He said she was a showgirl."

"Really?"

"Yes, she apparently danced at the Windmill, from time to time."

The notorious Windmill Theatre was home to a long-running nude revue whose manager boasted about staying open throughout the Blitz, as a patriotic duty to servicemen. It was one of the few theaters in London that Agatha had never frequented.

"Looks like the old, old story," the inspector said. "She was a showgirl, her looks started to slip, she took to the streets. Since the blackout began, prostitution's gone up like a barrage balloon—all along Haymarket and Piccadilly, the girls stand with their torches pointing down, lighting their feet, so clients can find them easily."

"I'm sure it passes the time," Agatha said dryly, "during a blackout."

Sir Bernard was kneeling at his Gladstone bag, which, unclasped, yawned wide; he was putting on rubber gloves.

The door to the adjacent apartment opened and a slender, not unattractive woman of perhaps twenty-five years stood, her hand with its red fingernails tight around the neck of her cotton terry cloth robe; a red-and-white candy-striped sash hugged her narrow waist. Despite the robe, she was fully (and rather overly) made-up.

Agatha hoped she was not making an unfair assumption by taking this young woman for another "working girl."

"I . . . I believe I've composed myself, Inspector. I could answer your questions now, I think."

The inspector glanced at Agatha. "This is Ivy Poole, Mrs. Mallowan. Miss Oatley's friend and neighbor."

Ivy Poole, her dark brown eyes huge, said, "Actually,

Inspector, Evelyn is a missus. Was a missus. Mrs. Oatley, she was. I'm a miss. Miss Poole."

The inspector wrote that down in a small notebook. Agatha removed the small spiral notebook from her topcoat pocket and began making her own minutes of the proceedings.

Miss Poole remained poised in her open doorway, leaning against the jamb; there was something sexual about the pose, and whether this was innate in the woman's nature or perhaps reflected her profession or was a method of trying to get on the inspector's good side, Agatha could not venture.

"And who might you be, dearie?" Miss Poole asked Agatha, with a frown.

The inspector answered for her: "This is my secretary. We both take notes, and compare them later. That's standard police procedure, Miss Poole. . . . Of course, you wouldn't know that, since I'm sure you've never had any run-ins with the law."

"I haven't, at that," she said. She had a pretty mouth but her teeth were crooked, up and down. "Got a fag?"

The inspector provided her with a cigarette and lighted it up for her.

Agatha wondered if the young apparent prostitute would be quite so casual if she could share the view that the mystery writer had: the mutilated corpse of the prostitute next door.

"Was Evelyn a working girl?" the inspector asked.

"Who am I to say? I have a job in a restaurant."

"Which restaurant?"

"Well, I used to have. I'm between engagements. But

Evie, she used to go out in the evenings, so draw your
own conclusions."

"Her husband doesn't live with her?"

"No. They're separated. Bill's his name, I think. He's
a salesman, working up north someplace."

"And she would go out in the evenings?"

"Yeah. She lost her job at the Windmill. I guess she
got too fat for 'em. These Yanks likes 'em skinny.
Anyway, she'd come back about eleven p.m., sometimes with a man. You know—after the public houses
shut."

"What about last night?"

Miss Poole blew out smoke through her nostrils, like
a dragon. "I weren't her baby-sitter."

"What did you see, Miss Poole?"

"Not a bleedin' thing."

"What did you hear, then?"

"Well . . . maybe I did see something, at that."

"Tell me."

"Last night I thought I'd wash my hair before I went
to bed." She put her free hand in her tousle of dark
curls, and gave the inspector the least convincing de-
mure smile Agatha had ever seen. "I come out on the
landing, see, to fill the kettle in the loo. While I was out
here, here comes Evie, up the stairs with a man. They
went into her room."

"What time was this?"

"I didn't set my clock by it."

"Take your best guess, Miss Poole."

"Eleven-fifteen, p'haps?"

"Can you describe the man?"

"There's just the one light. It's terrible dark out here."

"What did you see, Miss Poole?"

She shrugged, exhaled smoke. "You won't involve me in this, Inspector, will you? There's a good bloke."

"Miss Poole, you are involved. The woman who lives next door to you was murdered. You may have seen the man who did it. Wouldn't it behoove you to have that 'bloke' picked up and put away?"

She frowned. "You should hang the bleedin' bastard, is my opinion."

"And mine. Help me do that."

"Well. . . . He was a civilian. Medium height. Wearing a light-blue overcoat. Gray trousers. Tan shoes. No hat. That's all I can remember."

"You're doing fine, Miss Poole. What about his face?"

"Sorry. Didn't get a good look at that. Not much light out here, as I was sayin'."

"Well, you certainly took notice of his clothes."

"Well, guv, that's how a girl sizes up a man, ain't it?"

"All right. What happened then?"

She shrugged again, sighing smoke. "I stayed up till midnight, maybe a quarter after, give or take a tick. I have a little fireplace—I was sitting in front of the warm, brushing my hair, drying it. . . ." Another coquettish look at the inspector. "A girl has to look her best in these times, you know."

"What else, Miss Poole?"

"Well, I could hear Evie's radio going, next door. She did that sometimes, turned it way up, when she had gentleman guests. It's a way of . . . making so's I couldn't hear what went on over there. Only a thin partition-like, between rooms, you know. But I have a bigger place than Evie's, Inspector; bedroom's separate from the other room. You can come have a look, if you like . . ."

"Maybe later. Go on, please."

"Well. I went into my bedroom about twelve-fifteen, twelve-thirty. Can't hear the radio in there."

"Did you hear anyone leave the flat?"

"No. But even if she did, or he did, I wouldn't be able to hear it from my bedroom. I always shut my bedroom door, Inspector . . . and bolt it. Girl doesn't like to be interrupted."

No, Agatha thought, her eyes going to the open doorway framing the slain woman next door on the divan, *a girl doesn't. . . .*

"And anyway," Miss Poole said. "A girl's got to be careful around here. . . . Anything else, Inspector?"

"Not right now, thank you."

"Care for a cuppa? Hard-working public servant that you are?"

"No thank you."

She flashed him another fetching smile—perhaps just out of habit—and then the door shut and the inspector and Agatha were alone on the landing.

"Do you suspect the husband?" Agatha asked.

"Always. . . . We'll track him down."

Sir Bernard stepped into the hall, his rubber-gloved hands folded before him. "There is evidence we need to catalogue and collect, Inspector."

"What's your impression so far, Doctor?"

"My unofficial view, prior to autopsy?"

"Of course."

"She was partly strangled . . . but not enough to kill her. Whilst she was either semi-conscious or unconscious, the assailant cut her throat with a razor blade . . . it's on the bed."

"That's what killed her?"

"Almost certainly. The mutilations were post-mortem: twelve stab wounds with the point of a tin-opener . . . also on the bed . . . and five more with a set of curling tongs . . . on the bed, as well."

"Time of death?"

"Judging by the condition of the body, I place the killing between midnight and two this morning."

Agatha jotted this information in her notebook, then queried, "Before you begin to collect the evidence, the weapons, might I step inside the flat? I'd like to have a look. I'll take care."

The inspector and the pathologist exchanged prolonged glances; Sir Bernard nodded and Inspector Greeno said, "By all means, Mrs. Mallowan. But are you sure you wish to subject yourself to—"

"I am sure that I do."

Agatha entered the flat with the same reverence she would take with her into a chapel. This young woman, prostitute or not, was an innocent whose life had been savagely taken; the victim's terror, her pain, the final merciful unconsciousness . . . these Agatha sensed in the small, terrible, mundane space.

A cupboard had been broken into. A handbag and its scattered contents—including a wallet obviously emptied of its money—lay on a settee.

The victim herself was sprawled on the divan bed,

her head hanging over one side, a leg draped down over the other. Blood spattered the sheer nightgown; the naked flesh was very white. Agatha avoided the five-foot black pool. She noted the bloodstained can-opener on the bed, the bloody safety razor blade and the blood-stained pair of curling tongs.

And she looked at the face of the dead woman . . .

. . . and a hand involuntarily came, fingers curled, to the writer's agape mouth.

Collecting herself, Agatha exited quickly but carefully, and she took the inspector by the sleeve. The gesture caught him by surprise and he looked sharply at her.

"I know her," Agatha said.

"What?"

Sir Bernard's attention was on their guest, as well.

"Evelyn Oatley must be her real name," Agatha said, almost distractedly.

"Real name?" the inspector parroted.

"She had another," Agatha said, and glanced toward the dead woman. "Funny—she needn't have taken that client up to her flat last night. . . . Excuse me."

And Agatha went quickly down the street and out into the bracing air, where she drew in deep breaths, exhaling plumes.

Emerging behind her from the stairwell door, Inspector Greeno said, almost irritably, "Mrs. Mallowan, what are you saying?"

Without really knowing where she was going, Agatha clip-clopped down the street with the inspector tagging after. She ducked into a small cafe and ordered coffee while the perplexed if intrigued inspector took a seat across from her at a little table.

Finally Agatha cast her gaze upon him, and, smiling a little, albeit in a most melancholy manner, said, "She landed an understudy role just yesterday—she'd have been informed today. I saw her try out at the St. James Theatre, afternoon last . . . where she used the stage name Nita Ward."

FIVE

Privacy in a Public House

Agatha herself made the suggestion that those who'd witnessed Nita Ward's audition yesterday afternoon be interviewed today.

"I do not see them as suspects," Agatha told Inspector Greeno, as the pair sat in the tiny cafe, having coffee and tea respectively. She felt strangely self-conscious using the term "suspects" outside of the pages of fiction. "But at least one of my colleagues knew the poor girl prior to the audition, and the rest had direct contact with her."

"I'd like you to accompany me," the inspector said.

"I'm not sure that's wise—would my friends be as frank in front of me?"

Inspector Greeno twitched a humorless half-smile. "That's a good point, Mrs. Mallowan."

"I do wish you'd call me 'Agatha.'"

The grin had warmth and width that turned the bulldog face into something attractive. "Agatha it is—if you'll do me the honor of calling me 'Ted.'"

"Ted . . . what a wonderful designation . . . or should I say 'moniker,' out of respect for your trade? Such a cheery name for a homicide detective."

The inspector leaned forward, eyes narrow. "Here's my view of it—initially, they'll loosen up around you. Your presence will be a kind of reassuring factor. Then, after each interview, we'll exchange notes, so to speak. . . ."

She nodded. "I believe I understand. If at some point, my presence turns from comforting to inhibiting . . ."

"Then I'll question them again, at a later date, on my own. Rather more officially."

"These interviews, then, will be conducted unofficially. Informally."

"Absolutely, Agatha." He grinned again, though warmth wasn't part of it, this time. "We don't really think one of your theater people is the new Jack the Ripper, do we?"

"We don't. Particularly not the ladies."

Inspector Greeno raised an eyebrow. "Well, one never knows."

She frowned at him, curiously. "Aren't these sexually motivated murders?"

"Not necessarily. In all three, robbery has been at least a partial purpose—the previous victim gave up some eighty pounds to her slayer."

Agatha kept pressing. "But the savagery of the mutilation, in the region of Miss Ward's sexual organs . . ."

"A jealous woman could easily accomplish such a task."

The mystery writer's eyes flared. "I don't know about 'easily'. . . . What does Sir Bernard say about signs of sexual assault?"

"The first victim showed signs of sexual activity, but not the bruising and such usually associated with rape. . . . May I speak this frankly, Agatha?"

"You may. I will be insulted if you do not."

He waved a waitress over to request another cup of tea, and, once the girl had been dispatched, he said, "We have three victims, all female. The second one, our air-raid shelter schoolteacher, did not show signs of having had recent sexual activity. My guess is that Sir Bernard's examination of Miss Ward . . . Mrs. Oatley . . . will show that she did."

Agatha was nodding again, very slowly now. "I believe I follow you, Inspector."

"Ted."

". . . Ted. The first and third of the women, by the nature of their professions, would have had sexual intercourse, recently. Quite apart from the crime committed upon them."

The inspector also was nodding. "My best guess would be that our Ripper had 'normal' relations with victims one and three, after which—perhaps seized with some unnatural rage against women—he strangled them."

Could this be, Agatha wondered, *an individual who—upon sexual climax—felt guilt, or even revulsion? A sense of uncleanness . . . either about himself, or his paid partner, that sent him into a misogynistic fury?*

She said, "Then you do think this is the work of a man."

"Most likely. But remember, Agatha—one theory about the original, Whitechapel Ripper, never disproven, is that 'Jack' was a 'Jill.' "

Agatha found herself smiling. "Jill the Ripper? Isn't that absurd on its face?"

"Not really. The medical skills displayed by the turn-of-the-century Ripper were consistent with those of a midwife."

"From what I saw," Agatha said, and allowed herself a shudder, "our current Ripper, whether Jack or Jill, has no discernible surgical skills."

"I would have to agree. One does wonder . . . why has the killer escalated into mutilation? That is, if we are indeed looking at the same offender."

Agatha raised her eyebrows knowingly and sipped her coffee.

The inspector again leaned forward. "If you're thinking something, Agatha, please share it. I wouldn't be sitting here conversing with you in the midst of a murder case if I didn't take your contribution seriously."

"You're too kind . . . but I'm afraid my own prejudices would show through all too clearly, if I were to express this particular opinion."

"I'll take that into account."

Now Agatha leaned forward. "What has changed since the first two murders?"

"This one is more barbaric—"

"No. I didn't state myself clearly. What has changed between the first two murders and the *commission* of this third atrocity?"

The inspector frowned, then shook his head. "Nothing comes to my mind. What comes to yours?"

"The newspapers. Specifically, the tabloids."

The inspector's eyes flared. "Crikey! You're right. The press dubbed our boy a new 'Ripper.'"

"And how does our Ripper respond to this attention? He . . . or, giving you the benefit of the doubt, Ted, *she* . . . decided to live up to the title the press bestowed."

The bulldog face paled. "Surely that can't be. . . . The killer showed hatred of women in the first two killings, and he's merely getting bolder, and escalating out of his own mania . . . not spurred on by his press clippings."

Agatha shrugged. "It has been my observation that a certain breed of wrongdoer enjoys the limelight. No doubt this string of murders is the first 'important' thing this unfortunate individual has ever managed to do."

"Unfortunate?" His brow was heavily ridged with displeased surprise. "Surely, Agatha, you're not one of the 'reforming' breed, who think villains are *pooooor* victims of their heredity and environment . . . ?"

She took another sip; the coffee was wonderfully bitter. "I'm willing to believe that the likes of our Ripper are 'made' that way . . . born with a kind of disability, as if coming into this world blind."

"That hardly justifies—"

"One should *pity* them," she said, interrupting (something she seldom did, but the views she held on this subject were strong within her). "But *not* spare them."

He chuckled; the ridged forehead smoothed itself out. "Well, hearing that from you is a relief. Because if ever a villain needed to swing, this one does."

She shrugged. "I'm not against hanging. What else can we do with those who are tainted with hatred and ruthlessness? For whom other people's lives go for nothing?"

"Mrs. Mallowan . . . Mrs. Christie. You are not what I expected."

"Have you read Milton, Inspector?"

"As a schoolboy."

"How well do you remember it?"

"As well as the next bloke, I'd say."

"Satan wanted to be great, do you recall? He wanted power—he wanted to be God. He had no love in him, no . . . humility. He chose evil."

The inspector was shaking his head again. "Difficult to believe that the newspapers themselves, by glorifying the likes of a Ripper, could somehow encourage him. . . ."

"It's a pity the papers save their bad reviews for artists, and reserve their rave reviews for criminals."

That amused the inspector, who finished his tea and requested that Agatha give him the names of—and any insights she might have into—each of the individuals they would be interviewing this afternoon. She did this, and he dutifully jotted notes.

A dress rehearsal of her new play was scheduled for two p.m. at the St. James, and Agatha felt confident that the inspector's interviews with the appropriate parties—producer Bertram Morris, director Irene Helier

Morris, dialogue coach Francis L. Sullivan, and the producer's secretary, Janet Cummins—could be squeezed
in around the proceedings. This left only Stephen
Glanville and Janet's RAF pilot husband, who would
not be at the theater for an interview.

"We could call Stephen," Agatha said, "and arrange a
meeting for his Whitehall office, or at the Lawn Road
Flats, after work."

"Either would be fine—you're kind to suggest it."
The inspector rose, saying, "I'll take care of the bill
while you give him a call, if you would. Oh, and would
you ask Dr. Glanville what the best way is, to get ahold
of this young cadet? Seeing as how he's a superior of
the boy's."

The cafe had a public phone, which Agatha used.
Stephen was apparently fairly important at the Air Ministry, because it took her one switchboard operator and
two secretaries to make her way to him.

"Well, what a bizarre coincidence," Stephen said.
"That young woman the next victim . . . how terrible.
How tragic."

Stephen's words rang hollow, but that was to be expected: when someone one knows only slightly dies, the
news arrives with an abstract impact, devoid of the
emotion the loss of a close friend would bring.

"Frankly, dear," Stephen was saying, "I really don't
know that I would have anything of use for your inspector. . . ."

Rather than point out to Stephen that talking to the
police in a murder investigation was not optional,
Agatha said, "Would you speak to him, though? Just as

a favor to me. I'm the one that caused this inconvenience, after all."

"And how on earth is that?"

"Well, by recognizing the girl."

". . . Would six-fifteen be convenient?"

"It would. Could you stop by my flat?"

"Certainly. Is there anything else?"

"Actually, there is. Inspector Greeno is going to want to chat with Janet Cummins's young flier. Perhaps you could make a call and find out when and how that might best be arranged."

"I will. Does the inspector want to talk to young Cummins this afternoon, or shall I bring the information to our meeting at six-fifteen?"

"I would imagine the latter is fine. We'll be at the theater for the better part of the afternoon, I should think."

As it turned out, the interviews were not held at the theater. With a full dress rehearsal under way, nowhere in the theater—from the stalls to the dressing rooms—could be commandeered; even the offices were bustling with phone calls relating to last-minute preparations for Friday's big event.

Agatha suggested the Golden Lion, next door. The narrow, intimate pub possessed dark mahogany woodwork, an impressive wooden liquor rack behind the bar, and an elaborate stained-glass window that had been boarded over for the duration, for protection of itself and the patrons.

The manager—a small man with big opinions—knew Agatha by sight (and reputation); she had signed a copy of *Orient Express* for him, some months ago, and he was predisposed to theatrical people, since his pub was a haunt for that crowd.

So arranging the use of the upstairs dining room—it was now two-thirty and past the lunch hour—was an uncomplicated negotiation. The narrow stairway was at the right rear of the pub, its winding well well-decorated with photographs and illustrations of actors and actresses who'd performed next door at the St. James, over the last hundred years or so.

Inspector Greeno and Agatha set up shop at the table-for-four nearest the stairs.

Francis L. Sullivan—the tall, rather heavyset actor Agatha knew as Larry—was the first to be interviewed. As dialogue coach, he among their short list could slip away most easily, during dress rehearsal.

"Primarily," Larry said, his baritone sonorous even at its most casual, "I've been hired to work with the understudy for the ingenue—a replacement proved necessary, at this, the eleventh hour. This new girl hasn't even come around yet. They've only just notified her."

The inspector sat facing the interviewee, with Agatha to one side, her back to the wall. Ted Greeno had made it clear to Sullivan that this chat was informal and, when Larry asked if he might have a Guinness while they spoke, the inspector had assented.

"How terribly sad," the actor was saying, after a sip from his foaming mug. "I spoke to Miss Ward on stage, and backstage, as well. She was praying for this part. That's exactly what she said: praying."

"It was that important to her," the inspector said.

"Yes. She told me she'd done rather well, before the

war. Claimed she'd had speaking parts in a number of revues, and of course she had a nice little role in *The Dancing Years*."

Agatha said, "With Ivor Novello? Why, I saw that."

"I saw it, too," Larry said. "I remember her in it. She did fine for herself . . . but it was one of the plays that hit hard times as the war approached."

"The night I attended," Agatha mused, "the house was so thin, Ivor stepped out and invited the public from the gallery to occupy the vacant seats."

Larry nodded, causing his second chin to goiter a bit. "Poor kid said she'd been reduced to working the Windmill."

Agatha raised her eyebrows at the mention of the home of notorious nude revues. "I didn't see her perform *there*."

The inspector, lightly, asked, "How about you, Mr. Sullivan? Did you see her at the Windmill?"

His hand, lifting the mug of ale, froze halfway to his fully open mouth; the half-hooded eyes opened all the way, as well. The effect was not flattering.

"Why, no," Larry said. "I never frequent that kind of display. You see, I'm a happily married man, Inspector."

"I rather think any number of happily married men have been known to frequent the Windmill."

"Well," Larry said, shifting his massive frame in his hard wooden chair, "I'm not one of them."

"Did it occur to you," the inspector said, "that Miss Ward, in mentioning that she'd danced in a nude revue, might have been . . . approaching you?"

The big man blinked; he looked like a confused owl. "Approaching me . . . in what sense, sir?"

"Mr. Sullivan, the Ward girl was a prostitute."

But, surprisingly, this remark did not seem to unsettle the actor in the least. "So I gathered. A terrible thing, a pity, but some of these young girls, even formerly respectable actresses, down on their luck in these times . . . what with the servicemen flooding the city . . . well."

"Did you work with the girl last night?"

He set down the mug hard and it splashed a bit. "What? . . . Inspector, I'm starting not to like the sound of this. Agatha, would you tell the inspector I'm a respectable thespian. I played Poirot, for pity's sake!"

Not terribly well, Agatha thought, then said, "I don't think the inspector means to imply anything untoward, Larry."

"Certainly not," the inspector said. "But you yourself, Mr. Sullivan, indicated you were hired to work with the new understudy. And Miss Ward was selected as the new understudy, yesterday."

"Well, she was not informed of her good fortune," the actor said. "I believe our director was considering Miss Ward and another actress. Her selection would have been announced today."

"No offense meant, Mr. Sullivan," the inspector said cheerfully. "But you can see how I might assume you and the understudy may have worked together, yesterday night."

" 'Worked together'? Is that meant as a euphemism?"

"Working on her performance. On her lines. With the opening coming in just a few days . . . I'd imagine you theater folk labor at all sorts of odd hours."

"We do," Larry said, with strained dignity.

"By the way," the inspector said, "could you tell me where you were last night? How you spent the evening?"

Again the eyes widened, and he looked toward Agatha, as if for help. "This is starting to sound as though I'm a suspect."

Agatha smiled and shrugged. "I answered the same question, Larry."

His eyes beseeched her. "Agatha—how can you be party to this insulting interrogation? Tell him I'm a happily married man. Do you honestly think I would betray my darling Danae?"

In truth, she did not. She found Larry a dear man, and the affections of his attractive, younger wife Danae surely constituted all the rotund actor required in his romantic life. She recalled fondly time spent with the couple at their home in the country, at Haslemere, Surrey, set as it was against Spanish chestnut woods—truly delightful (not a bad setting for a mystery, she thought, filing the notion away and moving quickly on).

Still, Larry's wife was in the country and Larry was in the city. Further, thespians (as Larry would have it)— as much as Agatha adored them—were a breed unto themselves, and some of the most refined, elegant of them were alley cats, morally and sexually speaking.

She did not believe Larry fell into this class; but she could not say she would have been astonished to be proven wrong.

"Larry," Agatha said gently, "if you would be more comfortable speaking to the inspector, out of my presence. . . ."

"No! No." The big man shook his big head. "I have nothing at all to hide. I dined with friends at my hotel, the Savoy . . . I can provide a list . . . and then spent the rest of the evening alone, in my room."

"That's where you'd have been between eleven p.m. and two, say?"

"It is."

The inspector said nothing. Agatha could guess what thoughts were coursing through the detective's mind: this alibi was essentially no alibi; slipping out, unnoticed, from the Savoy in the middle of the night (and back in again) would not have been at all difficult to accomplish.

The inspector wrote down the names of Larry's dinner companions—a theatrical group numbering six, including Larry himself—and thanked the actor for his cooperation and help.

Somewhat flustered, Larry offered his hand to the inspector and, as they shook, said, "I certainly meant no offense. My apologies, if I appeared defensive. You caught me quite off-guard."

"Not all. . . . Oh, Mr. Sullivan?"

The actor was poised at the top of the stairwell, a foot dangling in midair; his expression reminded her of a startled deer in the woods. Poor dear.

"Would you mind sending Mr. Morris over? He indicated he should be free, by this time."

"Certainly. My pleasure. Good day, Inspector."

"Good day, Mr. Sullivan."

As usual, Bertie Morris was impeccably dressed—his dark gray suit went well with the lighter gray silk tie and off-white shirt. The handsome features framed by a balding, round head were solemn, and his tone was equally grave.

"I wish I could help you, Inspector," he said. "But I hardly knew the young woman. It's an awful thing. So very sad."

"My understanding, Mr. Morris," the inspector said, "is that you arranged for the audition. You must have known her."

"I did know her." To Agatha, Bertie asked politely, "May I smoke?"

"Certainly."

He withdrew a gold cigarette case and was lighting up as he said, "I had seen Miss Ward in *The Dancing Years*. She handled lines well."

"And she was attractive."

"Indeed she was."

"You're aware she was a . . . dancer at the Windmill."

"Many talented girls are reduced to that kind of thing, Inspector. Must I tell *you* of the hard realities of London? It's unfortunate. I was hoping to give her a . . . break."

"You didn't know her socially, then. You merely remembered her from a play you'd seen her in."

He exhaled smoke, away from Agatha. His hands, she noted, were slender, artistic; he wore a number of gold rings, one with a diamond. The wartime trend toward austerity of dress had not taken with Bertie.

"I did know Miss Ward, slightly. In a social manner."

Agatha glanced at the inspector, then said to the producer, "Bertie, if you'd be more comfortable without my presence—"

"No. I have nothing to hide." A tight, humorless smile appeared as a small slash in the midst of the round face. "I have a reputation for, shall we say, fraternizing with showgirls and actresses. It's exaggerated, but not entirely unearned."

Inspector Greeno sat forward, slightly. "What was your relationship with Miss Ward?"

"I would say 'relationship' rather overstates it, Inspector. I happened to bump into Miss Ward in Piccadilly last week. We spent a social evening together. Dined. Danced. I heard the story of her sad present situation. And she asked if I might keep her in mind, should something turn up in one of my productions."

"What night last week?"

"I believe Wednesday. My wife was rehearsing, and I'd had a long day, working on the production. And I just decided to take an evening for myself."

"I see. And that one . . . social evening with Miss Ward . . . was the only night you've spent with her."

Bertie's eyes flashed. "I did not use that phrase— 'spend the night with her.' We dined and danced during the blackout. Just two friends catching up a little."

"Then you had known her previously."

"Just in passing. An attractive girl in the theatrical game. It's a small world. A kind of a family."

"Then you didn't go to her flat, that night."

"Of course not."

The inspector made a few notes, then asked, "And last night—you didn't socialize with Miss Ward?"

"No. My wife and I dined at our club, Boodles, which is quite near our flat in Park Place. We spent a quiet evening together, both utterly exhausted from our labors. You may ask Irene for confirmation."

Inspector Greeno did.

Irene Helier Morris—looking haggard and wearing almost no make-up, and yet still beautiful, if starkly so, her short dark hair disarrayed—sat in white blouse and dark slacks, as if she'd been out riding and fallen from her horse.

"I have only ten minutes, Inspector," she said in that commanding contralto. She may have looked frazzled, but she was the epitome of self-control. "We're between acts."

Murders happened every day, Agatha wryly thought; opening nights were uncommon.

"We can keep this brief," the inspector said. "For now."

Irene sighed. "I don't mean to be cold about it. But I didn't know this woman. I saw her exactly once—yesterday, when she auditioned, and did a decent job of it."

"She won the role."

"Yes. But we hadn't notified her yet."

"Who takes care of that?"

"It's a call Janet would make. My husband's major-domo."

"Speaking of your husband, Mrs. Morris—or do you prefer Miss Helier?"

"Mrs. Morris is fine. I have a stage name, just as Mrs. Mallowan in writing has a, uh . . . what is it called, Agatha, darling? A byline. Speaking of my husband . . . go on."

"He tells us," the inspector said, his tone bland, "that he knew Miss Ward, slightly."

"Yes. . . . Might I borrow a cigarette?"

"Certainly," the inspector said, and took a deck of smokes from his suitcoat pocket and lighted her up using a match from a Golden Lion matchbook.

"Why is it," Irene asked rhetorically, "that one 'borrows' a cigarette, when there is absolutely no intention nor possibility of its return?"

As the inspector waved out the flame, Irene drew in smoke, held it, savoring it, then exhaled grandly.

"My husband has an eye for sweet young things . . . although I gather Miss Ward was neither sweet nor terribly young . . . if younger than I. But as I understand it, murder is a risk a harlot runs, isn't it? And she was a harlot, after all . . . Agatha, do I sound cruel?"

"You sound pragmatic."

Irene nodded. "Thank you. That is exactly what I am, where Bertie is concerned. I turn a blind eye to his little flings. It's one of the perks of being a producer. Casting couch, the Americans call it. And Bertie, well . . . he needs the reassurance. When he was a boy, he was slender and that glorious face of his attracted females like honey. Now that he's lost his hair and gained some pounds and some years . . . what's the harm, if he gets his ego stroked, now and then? As long as it's not serious."

"You were prepared," the inspector said slowly, "to hire . . . as an actress for your production . . . a woman you knew, or strongly suspected, to have had a relationship with your husband?"

"Relationship!" She gave out a single sharp laugh. "I am the only relationship in Bertie's life. I am the love and light of his life. I am sure he's feeling somewhat neglected these days, tied up with the production as I am, and a night with a Nita Ward would not surprise me."

"How did you spend last evening?"

"Our flat is in Park Place—near where you lived for a while, Agatha . . . around the corner from the Ritz, directly opposite Boodles. That's where we dined yesterday evening. Then we had a quiet evening at home. Drank some wine. Listened to dance music on the radio. Sat by the fire . . . terribly romantic."

The inspector pressed. "Might your husband have gone out, later, last night? Perhaps after eleven, even after midnight? After you were asleep?"

"I was up quite late, actually. Probably until two. It was all Mrs. Mallowan's fault."

Agatha sat forward, touching her bosom. "My fault, Irene?"

Irene exhaled smoke through her nostrils and smiled regally, eyes sleepy. "Completely yours. I was reading your new one—*Evil Under the Sun*? You simply must tell me who you based the actress on, darling. I have my theories. . . . Is there anything else, Inspector?"

"No. Not at the moment. . . . Shoo Mrs. Cummins our way, would you, Mrs. Morris?"

"With pleasure."

When the director had gone, Inspector Greeno turned to Agatha and asked, "Do you think she might be covering for her husband?"

Agatha asked, "Do you think he might be covering for his wife?"

He let out a weight-of-the-world sigh. "Morris says he just 'bumped' into Miss Ward in Piccadilly. Do you believe that?"

"I do."

"As he said, show business is a small world. A family."

"Yes. An incestuous one."

The inspector's eyes widened.

The brunette secretary/assistant, Janet Cummins, was highly cooperative, but had little to tell.

"I dealt with Miss Ward at the audition," she said, her blue eyes large and rather naive behind the lenses of the black-rimmed glasses, "and spoke to her in that regard, probably half a dozen times."

"But you'd never met her before?"

"No."

"I understand it was your job to call her and inform her that she'd landed the understudy assignment."

"That's right. Before we left the theater evening last, Miss Irene told me she'd decided on the Ward woman. I was to give her a call, next morning. This morning, that is."

"And did you?"

"Yes. About ten o'clock. A police officer answered. I said I had news for Miss Ward, and the officer said Miss Ward was indisposed."

Nicely understated of the officer, Agatha thought.

The inspector was asking, "Do you happen to know if your husband knew the Ward girl?"

"Gordon? I don't imagine so. He certainly said nothing to me about it."

The inspector flicked a look Agatha's way, indicating he'd had the same thought she had: if the pilot did recognize the girl auditioning on stage, he'd be unlikely to say as much to his wife.

Agatha filled the awkward silence with a question: "Janet, are you able to spend many evenings with your husband? What with him stationed here in London."

"Now and again, but lately, no. I've been so busy with the production, and the nights we haven't worked all hours, I've been simply spent."

The inspector asked, "How about last evening? Were you and your husband together?"

"No. We talked about it, but I was exhausted. The last days before opening night are punishing. We talked about going out tonight, too, but Gordie's on fire duty."

"What does that consist of?"

"Staying in his billet, keeping himself available, should he be needed."

Agatha saw the wheels turning in the inspector's eyes—he could go out and talk to Cadet Cummins tonight.

"Is there anything else, Inspector? I really should get back."

"No, you've been very helpful, Mrs. Cummins. Thank you."

When they were alone, the inspector asked, "What do you make of that, Agatha? Anything strike you strange about any of our interviewees?"

She shook her head. "I can't say, really. How odd, to be faced with my friends and colleagues as if they were suspects in one of my fictions."

"I'm not sure they are suspects. We have a spree killer here, a multiple murderer. What we've heard this afternoon might constitute the makings for suspicions were Nita Ward the only victim."

Agatha nodded. "On the other hand, Ted, everyone we spoke to most certainly read at least some of the press coverage of the first two murders . . . the same 'Ripper' rabble-rousing rubbish we referred to earlier."

"That's true. But what strikes you as significant about that?"

"Well . . . I hesitate to say."

"No, please!"

"It will sound foolish. . . . It's a notion straight out of my books."

"I like your books. Try me."

"I was just thinking . . . if one wanted to commit a murder, and have it go undetected . . . what better way than to hide it among a series of killings by a madman?"

His eyes tightened and he began to nod, apparently taking her suggestion seriously, or at least pretending to. "The term the Americans use for that kind of thing is a 'copycat' killing."

"Really?" she said brightly.

And Agatha wrote that down.

In Agatha's tiny living room, the inspector sat on a comfortable chair while Agatha took a straightbacked one,

with Stephen Glanville sitting on the sofa, arms out-
stretched along the cushions on either side of him, his
legs crossed. He was the picture of casualness.

"With all due respect, Inspector," Stephen said, with
unhidden amusement, "this line of questioning indicates my good friend here has led you astray."

Agatha sat up. "Whatever do you mean!"

Stephen chuckled. "She's undoubtedly portrayed me
as some overaged Casanova, constantly in pursuit of
one romantic conquest after another."

Frowning, the inspector said, "She's done nothing of
the kind . . ."

"Oh, I don't mean to get your dander up, Inspector . . . or yours, for that matter, Agatha. But I am a married man, and I have had a few ill-advised affairs."

Agatha rose. "Why don't I step into the library, while
you and Inspector Greeno continue . . ."

"Nonsense," Stephen said, waving for her to sit back
down, which she did. "I'm not going to embarrass anyone but myself . . . and I have a rather high embarrassment threshold, as you may have noticed."

"I simply asked," the inspector said, "if you had
known Nita Ward."

"And my point," the handsome professor replied, "is
that my occasional peccadilloes not withstanding, I do
not necessarily know every shop girl, chorine and
streetwalker in the city of London. . . . No, I saw Miss
Ward only once, when she auditioned yesterday. And
barely took note of that."

"And yesterday evening—"

"I was in my flat, reading up on the Eleventh Dynasty. Agatha, if you will take the time to read the Henanakhte Papers, I just *know* you'll come around."

The inspector flashed a look at Agatha, who sighed and said, "Stephen is twisting my arm about writing a mystery set in ancient Egypt."

Brightly, Stephen said, "It's a dreadful alibi, I know, Inspector. I was alone. The Windmill chorus line wasn't available for a private function, last night, I'm afraid."

The Inspector tried to sit straight up, but the comfortable armchair worked against him. "Sir, this is a serious matter. I can't say I appreciate the frivolity of your attitude."

Stephen's smile faded. "I do apologize. I've had a long day, and—meaning no disrespect at all to the late Miss Ward—have been dealing with life and death matters relating to the war, and our young men who are so gravely at risk. That you would drag me into this, simply because of my 'reputation,' is the height of absurdity, and rather than be insulted about it, I decided to be amused."

The inspector, who'd also had a long day, rose and nodded. "Point taken. . . . Did you have an opportunity to inquire about Cadet Cummins?"

Stephen rose. He withdrew a small folded piece of paper from his suitcoat's inner pocket. "Here's the address of Cummins's billet, and the names of various superior officers. You might catch him tonight—he's on fire picket."

"His wife said as much. I'll do that."

Agatha had also risen. She stood between the two men, and placed a hand on their nearest arms, rather like a benign referee.

"I believe I'll allow you to make that call by yourself, Inspector," she said. "I've had quite enough detecting for one day, I'm afraid."

"Understood, Mrs. Mallowan."

Suddenly playing host, Stephen said, "I'll see Inspector Greeno to his car, my dear," and took the man by the elbow and walked him to the door and outside.

Poised in the doorway, she watched as—beyond the breast-high brick pillars bookending the wrought-iron gate—a quite serious Stephen Glanville conversed with Inspector Greeno, whose demeanor was equally somber, though this was a respectful exchange, not an argument.

When the inspector had driven off in his Austin, Stephen returned to the porch.

"Your behavior," she said, "was quite despicable."

"I had nothing to guide me—I've never been a murder suspect before."

She could see in his face the wear and tear of his current life—the pressures of Whitehall, the complications of life away from his family—and knew how false the levity had been.

Suddenly she knew what he'd been speaking to Greeno about: once again, doubtless, Stephen had been pleading the case against Agatha's involvement in this investigation.

"You *are* worried about me, aren't you?" she said, and touched his sleeve.

A devilish half-smile flashed. "Careful—remember what a rogue I am with the ladies. . . . Shall we dine at the Lawn Flats restaurant, my dear? The off-the-rations special is baked cod and parsnip balls."

She winced. "Hitler's secret weapon," she said.

But she got her coat and went with him.

February 11, 1942

And so, joining the gloom-driven hazards of the blackout, among the other strains and inconveniences of wartime, came this new and yet all too familiar terror.

The press, the tabloids in particular, seemed to take bloodthirsty relish in having so traditional and homegrown a menace to share with their readers; it was as if the yellow journalists were relieved to be able to interrupt the continuing chronicle of international woe—Singapore falling, Rommel's Afrika Corps advancing again in the Western Desert—with good old-fashioned British blood lust.

Any respectable women—forced to walk alone down pitch-dark snowy streets, making their way to the safety of air-raid shelters—moved quickly, looking about them in bird-like anxiety, terrified that a lurking murderer might spring from the silence of a doorway or an alley's *mouth, to claim another victim. And was a shelter truly safe, when Monday's victim had been discovered in one?*

And what of the not-so-respectable women of London?

The first Jack the Ripper had terrorized the East End, notorious in its day for an abundance of ladies of the evening. The Blackout Ripper—as the tabloids had dubbed the unknown killer, who had instantly become a household name—sought his soiled-dove prey on the West End, which had become (in these war years particularly, and in the words of Superintendent Fabian of the Yard) "the Square Mile of Vice."

Even before the blackout, the limited visibility of which made conditions virtually identical to Jack's fog-shrouded atrocities, these narrow streets and shadowy pavements—Soho, particularly—echoed with the eerie footsteps of London's long, proud, wicked criminal history. Here you could enjoy anything and everything, for a price—drugs, games of chance, blue movies (in "secret" cinemas); you could buy a diamond ring for two hundred and fifty pounds (only it would prove to be diamothyst, worth one-thirtieth of the price). You could be dominated by a woman with a whip, or defile a "virgin" (Catholic school girl costumes were a must, in the wardrobes of the higher-paid call girls).

By day and night, Piccadilly Circus was bustling, swarming with uniforms from many nations—Poles, Canadians, Free French, and of course the Americans, so many Americans. Sinful business was booming. . . .

So the women of the street, who were not seeking the relative safety of a shelter, put themselves at even greater risk than usual. Many stayed in, however, alone in their dingy flats—or confining their clientele to known and trusted "regulars"—too frightened to venture into their usual haunts. Unbeknownst to them, the ladies of the evening were joined by policewomen in plainclothes and too much make-up, under the watch of Yard men also in the disguise of ordinary clothing.

This had been Detective Chief Inspector Ted Greeno's doing, only one of a number of strategies he'd pursued, following the three murders. He was, after all, in charge of the biggest case of the war, the kind of murder case that could make a career.

Or break it.

SIX

A Quiet Morning

Agatha awoke with a start, slightly after seven a.m. Typically, she had been sleeping with her head under a pillow.

This was a wartime habit for her, a precaution against flying broken glass, and to help dampen the shrill cry of air-raid sirens, which she ignored. Since the war had begun, during air raids, she and Max had always stayed in their bedroom, wherever they might be living, and did not follow the conventional wisdom of fleeing to the basement.

The futility of shelters had been proven beyond doubt to Agatha when Sheffield Terrace had been bombed, one weekend, while she and Max were away in London. A bomb hit across the way, taking out three houses, and what had been blown up at their own home? The basement! The ground and first floors had gone largely undamaged (although her precious Steinway had never been quite the same).

Even before that incident, she refused any suggestions that she ought to go to a shelter. Few things frightened Agatha Christie Mallowan, but the thought of being buried alive, of being trapped underground under dirt and rubble . . . well, she had decided to sleep only in her own bed, wherever she might be.

And Max had honored her preference, staying right with her throughout the nastiest and noisiest of bombings. By now she was so used to air raids on London that she hardly woke up for them, sleeping through the worst of it in 1940. When a siren or bomb did manage to wake her, she'd merely roll over, muttering, "Oh, dear, there they are again!" and would pull the pillow over her head, tighter.

What had woken her, this morning, was that nightmare again, that damned Gunman dream. She dreamed she was having lunch with Max in a large country house, surrounded by flower beds. Afterward, she and Max walked through the garden, vivid colors, wonderful fragrances, all around them, James on a leash at her side; and then she had glanced at Max and, suddenly, he was that blue-eyed Gunman, and rather than suffer any longer through the unpleasantness of it, she had forced herself awake. Right now!

Next to her bed, as was also her wartime habit, was a chair on which she kept her two most precious possessions: her fur coat; and her rubber hot-water bottle. Gold and silver came and went; but in this war, rubber, now that was valuable.

The fur coat and rubber hot-water bottle, she knew, would see her through all emergencies.

Outside her window, the world was an overcast gray, the sky the color of gunmetal and her beloved cherry tree a skeletal figure silhouetted against the sky like a surrendering prisoner. She had intended to sleep in, but once awake, she was awake . . .

She felt rather in a funk and did not care to dress straightaway, much less go down for breakfast in the little Lawn Road Flats restaurant. Even the most trivial passing conversation with a waitress or fellow resident of the Flats seemed quite more than she could bear to face. She was scheduled to work this evening at the hospital, in the pharmacy, and so the day stretched out endlessly before her. Slipping into the lovely powder-blue Jaeger dressing gown Max had given her as a farewell present, she padded downstairs.

She did not bathe—she was restricting herself to twice a week, due to the water shortage—but allowed herself a sponge bath, using soap sparingly, as the ration was one tablet per person per month. (When she did bathe, she used only the allowed five inches of hot water; it was the least she could do, since King George VI was having his valet measure five inches thereof for the royal bath.) She put on no make-up, briefly frowning at the face of the old woman who glanced at her from the mirror.

After poaching herself an egg and making toast and coffee, and barely touching any of it, she wandered into the library and sat herself down. She began to cry. She wept for perhaps five minutes. This had happened before, and she kept a handkerchief handy in a pocket of the robe.

She was not sure why she was blue ("depressed" would have overstated it). Missing Max was a constant in her life, but on certain days, his absence hit her like a physical blow; she hurt from not having him here—she ached with the possibility of any harm coming to him. True, he was as safe as any military man might be, in his posting; but this was, nonetheless, war. People died.

She might die. A bomb might strike the Flats and her pillow wouldn't do a bit of good and she and Max would never see each other again. She cried a little more.

James was curled beside the chair, but the terrier ran for cover when she dried her face, blew her nose, cleared her throat, rose with resolve, moved to her desk and began typing—the machine's chatter always frightened the animal, though on the last air raid, the dog had slept soundly through it, much as he did through thunderstorms.

She typed a letter to Max, not telling him anything of her true-crime research project with Sir Bernard Spilsbury. Max would probably have approved of the effort, had he been around; he was always supportive, and as a man whose calling in life was digging for truth, he would not likely echo Stephen Glanville's rather chauvinistic concerns regarding a mere woman undertaking an endeavor at all dangerous.

But she did not want to burden Max with what she was up to, nor did she want to risk him reacting, well, like a normal husband . . . the distance between them, in these times already fraught with peril, might cause Max to revert to conventional male wisdom (if the latter two words weren't a contradiction in terms).

Agatha did admit to her absent husband that she was "sad this morning, and had cried a bit." She thanked him for his letters, his many loving letters, and admitted to him that receiving such tender missives "after all these years we have been married makes me feel that I have not been a failure in life—that at least I have succeeded as a wife."

She paused, embarrassed. And then she said to herself: *He is your husband. You need not hide from him.*

And she went on: "What a change now, from the unhappy, forlorn person you met in Baghdad so many years ago. You have done *everything* for me, my love."

She went on to tell him about the play, and how well rehearsals were going, and that she was dreading opening night, and yet there was something terribly brave of presenting a first night in Blitz-ravaged London. It seemed to her British in the best sense.

When she'd finished the letter (three typewritten pages) and prepared it for mailing, she moved to her comfortable chair, taking a sheaf of papers with her.

The galley proofs of her novel, *The Body in the Library*, had arrived yesterday from her publisher, William Collins & Sons. They had rebounded well, after their offices were bombed in December 1940, though the sorry state of their records had contributed to her current financial difficulties. The Collins book warehouse in Paternoster Row near St. Paul's had been ravaged as well, and publishing remained dicey, what with paper allocations cut to a fraction of pre-war quantities.

So the rest of the morning was spent checking for punctuation and typographical problems in the latest Jane Marple mystery. She found herself liking Miss Marple and quite satisfied with the book—a rarity, as she was a harsh critic of her own work—and her mood brightened.

She did pause, at one point, to get up and go out to the kitchen for an apple. James followed her and she gave him half a biscuit (even dogs were on ration) and then she realized why she'd been so forlorn.

It hadn't been Max, not entirely. . . .

That crime scene yesterday—she had viewed it dispassionately, with the clinical perspective of a nurse, with the calloused attitude of a war correspondent. Not once had she felt ill or in any way uncomfortable. It had not been a pose; it had come naturally to her.

But now, as she settled back into her little flat where she'd been writing her homicidal confections—hiding away from the war and her absent husband—the loss of life represented by that woman's brutal murder hung over her like a cloud, rumbling, dark, oppressive, with the promise of a storm.

For a moment she sat in her comfortable chair, James again curled beside her (now that the machine-gunning of the typewriter had been silenced), the loose pages of her latest mystery in her lap, and wondered if she should remove herself from the investigation. Already she had involved her friends and colleagues, and—while she of course knew her responsibility had been to aid the police in their efforts—she felt embarrassed by the inconvenience she had caused them.

The irony was, Agatha enjoyed the company of the theatrical crowd precisely because their existence was somehow disconnected from real life. She found it relaxing to associate with actors in wartime, because to these children—whose profession was acting out fantasies—the theatrical world *was* the real world. This ravaged London where the war was happening was an incomprehensible nightmare, a long, drawn-out inconvenience preventing them from going on with their own truly important lives.

All they spoke of was the theater—of fellow actors and directors and producers; the only momentous events taking place in the world were those happening in the theatrical world. The only war talk related to the Entertainments National Service Association.

She had found this wonderfully refreshing.

And now she had ruined everything by introducing a murder—a real murder—into the playacting.

This thought had barely passed through her mind when the telephone rang. She had a sudden chill that had nothing to do with the winter weather: *if that were Sir Bernard or Inspector Greeno, it would likely mean another young woman had been murdered.*

If so, would she politely withdraw from her association with the investigators? Or would she answer the call?

Well, she would answer this call, at least. She rose, pausing to pick up her spiral notebook and a pencil, and went to the phone on its stand by the stairs.

And it was indeed Inspector Greeno.

"Oh, Ted," she said, "I hope there hasn't been another killing."

"There hasn't," the pleasantly gruff baritone voice responded. "At least, not that we know of. And I've practically jumped, all morning, every time the phone's rung, dreading another such discovery."

Somehow it was reassuring that she and the hard-boiled inspector had been thinking, and reacting, alike.

The inspector had called, "just checking in," but with a good deal of new information for her. For one thing, he had a new telephone number for her reference.

He had set up his enquiry headquarters in an office at the Tottenham Court Road Police Station, out of which he was supervising a systematic scouring of Paddington and Soho. All of the "top resources of Scotland Yard" had been mobilized, and every available man from the wartime-depleted police force had moved into the West End. A circular with the description of Evelyn Oatley's last gentleman caller, as provided by nextdoor neighbor Ivy Poole, had already been widely distributed.

"We're talking to every known prostitute," he said, "and asking each girl if she's met a violent client in the blackout, of late, or if she knows of another girl who has."

There was a small chair by the telephone stand; Agatha sat. "Has this proved fruitful?"

"To an extent, but so far everything falls into that latter category—girls who've heard stories from other girls. All quite second-hand."

"Enough to go on, though, I would hope."

"Two promising leads. We've heard complaints of a 'rough customer' who passes himself off as the illegitimate son of a member of the House of Lords. Speaks in an affected, imitation Oxford accent, and demands to be called the 'Duke.' "

"Does he have a real name?"

"Not that he's ever given to any of these good-time girls, and their descriptions are vague and inconsistent. He's a good-looking fellow, that much they all agree on— but he's been variously described as twenty-five and thirty-five and points in between. Very well-dressed, as befits his pretensions. Tosses money around. He's blue-eyed and brown-eyed and, well, you can see the problem."

"Could his story about a noble if illegitimate heritage be true?"

"Possibly, but more likely it's simply a fantasy he's hiring these girls to help him enact. That's rather typical of working girls and their 'mugs.' "

"You said 'two promising leads.' What's the other?"

"Ah, well. A girl named Phyllis O'Dwyer is said to have had a 'close call' or a 'scrape' with a particularly wild customer. Three of her friends told us the same story."

"What does Phyllis say?"

"Apparently, she's holed up somewhere. Frightened out of her skin. We are looking for her."

"That does sound promising." Agatha was making notes. The inspector didn't seem to mind answering her questions, so she pressed on. "Has Sir Bernard uncovered any significant evidence?"

"Well, he's made his opinion official that no sexual assault was involved in any one of the three cases. And he passed along to Superintendent Cherrill various items for fingerprinting."

Fred Cherrill was to fingerprinting what Sir Bernard Spilsbury was to forensics: the Yard was taking no chances on this case. Top resources, indeed.

"Going back to the Evelyn Hamilton murder," Inspector Greeno said, "the superintendent checked the handbag that had been emptied out in the air-raid shelter, and various contents of the bag; but he found only the victim's prints."

"I hope Superintendent Cherrill did better with that tin-opener and those curling tongs."

"Smudged prints only, I'm afraid—but he was able to back up Sir Bernard's opinion that our assailant is left-handed: the tin-opener had a smeared print belonging to the little finger of a left hand. The tongs had also been held in a left hand, and a mirror in the emptied-out handbag had a left thumbprint. Again, not identifiable, but indicating we indeed have a left-hander."

Agatha paused in her note-taking. She said, "Ted . . . Inspector . . . I must say it's generous of you to take time to share all of this with a . . . what is the word? Kibitzer?"

"Agatha, I have orders from the Home Office to give you every courtesy. But beyond that, you've been enormously helpful in this inquiry, thus far—not only with the theatrical link-up, but with your keen powers of observation."

"Again, all I can say is, you're most generous. Frankly, I'm blushing." But, of course, she wasn't. "Have you had any luck tracing Mrs. Oatley's husband?"

"In fact, we have. Our people traced him to Blackpool. He seems in the clear. His alibis on the murder nights are, as you say in your books, ironclad."

She chuckled. "Well, most of the 'ironclad' alibis in my books are in the possession of the murderer."

"Not in this case, I'd wager. The bloke and his wife have been separated by mutual agreement for over a year. They've stayed friendly, far as it goes, and he's seen her in London, from time time . . . most recently, about a week ago."

"Was he aware of his wife's profession? And I am not referring to dancing or acting."

"Mr. Oatley says not. I don't believe him."

"Well . . . that's the kind of lie that does not raise suspicions."

"True enough. But the main reason I called, Agatha, was to give you a report on your friends at the theater. We've checked up on all of them."

"Now I feel quite ashamed of myself."

"Please don't. I can give you mostly good news about all of them—their stories, their alibis, all check out."

"Then why, Ted, do you say 'mostly' good news?"

The inspector's sigh came across the wire distinctly. "It's the problem detectives have, outside of books, where alibis are concerned—people rarely have those ironclad ones we mentioned, before."

"You mean, it's difficult to determine whether Larry Sullivan sneaked out of the Savoy and back in again? Too many exits?"

"Yes, and not enough doormen—only at the front and back. There are numerous side and rear ways out of the hotel. Most of the doors lock automatically, but one could arrange easily enough for a door not to shut entirely or place adhesive over a lock."

She nodded to herself. "And Bertie and Irene's, with their quiet evening at home, is also rather worthless, isn't it?"

"Yes. One could be covering for the other. And your friend Stephen Glanville says he was home, alone, at his flat, which is where Janet Cummins spent the evening, as well."

She knew the detective meant Janet had spent the evening in her own flat, and did not correct him.

"Men of mine," he was saying, "attempted to find witnesses who might have seen Mr. Glanville or Mrs. Cummins exit their buildings, but without success."

"And what about Mr. Cummins? Janet's handsome cadet? Aren't military men often the clients of these 'good-time girls'?"

The inspector grunted. "He's in the clear, too. I spoke to him at his quarters last night—he was on fire duty, as you may recall. He seems an intelligent, well-spoken lad."

"He wasn't acquainted with the late Mrs. Oatley, or should I say Miss Ward?"

"No. Cadet Cummins says he saw her only that once, on stage, trying out for the understudy part."

"And what exactly puts him 'in the clear'?"

"Our RAF cadet was in billets at the time of the two recent murders. The billet passbook confirms the times he came and went, and his roommates verified seeing him go to bed and get up in the morning."

"I must say I'm relieved."

"And why is that?"

"Well, I like the young man. He has excellent taste, you know."

"Really? How do you know that, Agatha?"

"He's a fan of my books."

Inspector Greeno actually laughed; she had a feeling it might have been his first laugh of the day.

He said, "Frankly, Agatha, I don't find it likely that one of your theatrical crowd is our Ripper . . . whether Jack or Jill. I find it marginally possible that one of them might have had reason to kill Miss Ward, or should I say Ms. Oatley . . . but the other two murders? No."

"And you find my notion of a murderer hiding his work amid another murderer's tally . . . melodramatic. More suited to Hercule Poirot's world than Ted Greeno's."

"I do," he admitted. "Nonetheless, the Yard is . . . as I said . . . mobilizing all its top resources. And you are a top resource in my book, Mrs. Agatha Mallowan."

"How can I be of help?"

"Stay with us, on the scent."

"You think there will be more murders, then?"

"I'm surprised this morning's phone hasn't rung. I'm wondering if some poor girl is dead on her divan, right now . . . as yet undiscovered by a meter man or landlord."

"Why are you so certain, Ted?"

"Two murders in two days . . . with the savagery of them mounting. This is a beast, Agatha. A beast on a killing spree. If you should want to bow out of it, I would not blame you. I would understand."

"Oh, I do want to bow out of it."

Surprise and disappointment colored the inspector's voice. "You do?"

"I do . . . but I won't."

And they rang off; and both went off to work, on their respective murder cases.

February 12, 1942

Her mother was expecting her.

That was what confused Mary Jane Lowe, who had taken the tube from Charing Cross station to meet her mother, Margaret, at the second-floor flat on Gosfield Street, a narrow side street just off Tottenham Court Road. Mary Jane was fourteen, a tall, dark, brown-eyed brunette with a blossoming figure the boys were noticing; right now she was boyishly dressed herself—navy blue coveralls and a matching corduroy jacket—partly because that was the style, but also due to the chill, snowy weather.

Mary Jane did not wear make-up—her mother didn't approve—but her features were so pretty, her brown eyes so big and long-lashed, her smile so wide and white, her lips so full, she didn't really need to. She was proud of her good looks, which she'd inherited from her mum, who had just enough Spanish blood in her to make both mother and daughter seem vaguely exotic.

Someday, perhaps, she would be as beautiful as her mother.

Before the war, Mary Jane's mum had kept a boardinghouse in the coastal town of Southend, and the girl had fond, vivid memories of sunny blue-sky mornings and running along the sand with their Scottie terrier. But Southend tourism was a thing of the past these days—barbed wire strung along the beach, aimed to keep out the invading German hordes, kept out holiday funseekers, as well—and then the boardinghouse, which was on the verge of going broke anyway, got commandeered by the military.

Mum had left Mary Jane in Southend with Uncle Rodney and Aunt Grace—whose restaurant business had survived, thanks to the soldiers—and, while Mary Jane carried on with school and all, Mum had found a position as a banker's secretary, in London.

This, at least, was what Mary Jane's mother had told her. But Mary Jane had suspicions otherwise. First, Uncle Rod and Auntie Grace gave each other funny looks, whenever Mary Jane—receiving monthly envelopes of cash from London—commented on Mum's secretarial situation. And Mary Jane herself knew Mum had never had anything like training in that line of work.

She wondered if Mum were a waitress or a cleaning woman or such like, and was ashamed to say so to her little girl, particularly after they'd had such a nice life at the Seaside Inn. She also wondered, sometimes, if her late father had really died when Mary Jane was two; she was at an age where the thought did occur to her that her father, who was just a grinning face in some faded photographs, might have simply run off and left Mum and her to fend.

When the girl came to London, once every six weeks or so, to spend a weekend with Mum (and Scottie, who Uncle Rod had not welcomed), Mary Jane longed to ask her mother these and other related questions. But somehow Mary Jane could not bring herself to do so. Mum seemed so sad, these days.

Funny thing was, Mum didn't say she was sad or act sad, and in fact, around Mary Jane, she smiled rather too much, if anything. Mary Jane sensed something forced about Mum's good mood, and her over-involved anecdotes about herself and co-workers at the bank, and how she was the bank president's "right-hand gal."

Now, as she knocked on the door for the twentieth time, with Scottie on the other side, yapping and yowling (despite the girl's assurances: "It's only me, love"), Mary Jane trembled with an intermingling of frustration and fear. . . .

Outside the door, next to where Mary Jane had set down her little tan suitcase, was a wrapped parcel addressed to her mother. Its presence, this late in the day, on the doorstep, struck Mary Jane as odd.

Mum had said in her letter that she'd be taking Thursday and Friday off, to spend with Mary Jane, who had a long weekend because of end of exams. Staying in

Mum's flat was always rather harrowing—it seemed to Mary Jane little more than a glorified prison cell, really.

Mum said nice rooms were hard to come by, 'cause of the war and all, though Mary Jane suspected her mother was living so close to the bone so's she could send Mary Jane (and her uncle and aunt) all that money. But the girl always had a wonderful time, visiting Mum, and this weekend would be no exception. They would do all sorts of fun things together—take Scottie to the park, go to the cinema, perhaps spend an afternoon at Harrod's, pretending they could afford to buy something.

But with an unclaimed parcel on Mum's doorstep, and no response to ardent knocking, and Scottie going simply mad barking, Mary Jane felt herself teetering on the edge of panic. She knew she was being silly, but she couldn't help imagining the most tragic things . . . particularly with what the newspapers were saying about a Blackout Ripper and all. . . .

Absurd! Ridiculous! That fiend targeted streetwalkers, not bank secretaries . . . or waitresses, even, or charwomen. Her mum had simply got called away, had to go in for work, last minute. Probably the bank president himself. How could Mum say no to him?

Not sure what else to do, Mary Jane knocked on the door of the neighboring flat, Scottie's yapping sounding pitiful now.

The woman who answered was pretty, in a haggard sort of way, and was wearing a dark blue dressing gown; her platinum hair was up in pin curls, and she seemed to have just about applied half of her make-up—one eye, a beauty mark and her roughed-in lip rouge. She had a cigarette in one red-nailed hand and smoke curled like a question mark.

"Excuse me, ma'am," Mary Jane said, for she had never met her mother's neighbor before, "but I'm Mrs. Lowe's daughter, here for a visit . . ."

"I'm Alice Wick. You must be Mary Jane! The good student I keep hearin' so much about. Pearl's right proud of you."

"Pearl? My mother's name is Margaret."

"Just a nickname, love. Whatever's wrong?"

When Mary Jane had finished explaining, the neighbor frowned and said, "Y'know, love, I noticed that parcel there, myself, this mornin'."

"She might just not be back from the bank, yet. . . ."

Miss Wick frowned. "Was she goin' to the bank, dear?"

"That's where she works."

"Is it now? . . . Let me slip somethin' on, and we'll go find ourselves a constable."

And within minutes a bobby was shouldering open the door to the flat, and the little dog flew onto the landing and jumped into Mary Jane's arms, the girl kneeling to meet the dog halfway. She looked up and into her mother's sparsely furnished one-room flat—no sign of Mum. On the bed, which hugged the wall lengthwise, a black comforter bulged, probably with tangled bedclothes. At the foot of the bed, some of her mother's apparel was scattered, a dress, her coat, a little feathered hat.

Some other things were distributed around on the throw rug, near the side of the bed, but Mary Jane couldn't make out what they were, exactly. She caught a glimpse of steel catching light from somewhere, though the curtains were drawn.

Funny. Her mother usually kept the tiny flat tidy—a holdover from her landlady days.

It just didn't look . . . proper in there, somehow. The very stillness of the flat seemed unsettling to the girl.

"Officer," Mary Jane said, as the little dog licked her face eagerly, "would you mind terribly, going in and checking for me?"

"I was going to insist, miss," the bobby said, holding up his hand as if conducting traffic. "So if you'll just wait here. . . ."

The constable had an oval face with dark eyes set too close together, and wasn't much taller than Mary Jane, a fact amplified by the tin hat he wore in place of the traditional tall helmet. He couldn't have been much older than twenty. But his voice was both kind and firm, and he had a commanding way about him.

He entered the flat and Mary Jane saw him go to the bed and—though his back was to her, she could tell what he was doing—lifted up the black quilt. His head was bowed as he studied whatever it was on the bed; then he gently lowered the quilt and slowly—watching where he was going—came back out, his face very white.

"Mary Jane," the bobby said, his voice soft, kind, which oddly enough frightened her, "that's your name, isn't it? Mary Jane?"

"It is."

"Mary Jane, could you wait next door, with your pup, for a few minutes?"

He looked toward the neighbor, who nodded her assent; Miss Wick was wearing a white and pink housedress now, but her platinum locks were still in pin curls.

Then to the girl, the constable said, "There seems to be a problem in your mother's flat."

"What kind of a problem? What was under the quilt?"

The bobby turned to the blonde neighbor. "Do you have a phone, miss?"

"No."

"I'll use the box 'round the corner, then. Neither of you are to go into that flat. Is that understood?"

Miss Wick nodded.

He repeated it to Mary Jane: "Is that understood, miss?"

"Yes, sir."

Miss Wick slipped her arm around Mary Jane's shoulder; the girl was cradling the terrier in her arms like a baby.

The bobby's footsteps were echoing down the stairwell as Mary Jane entered Miss Wick's flat.

"Everything will be all right, love," Miss Wick said, again and again, as she paced and smoked and occasionally looked at the wall separating this flat from the next. Early on she asked Mary Jane if she wanted a glass of water—"It's all I have that's suitable, dear, I'm afraid"—and Mary Jane politely declined the offer.

Sitting on the couch, playing with the terrier, Mary Jane pretended to herself that her mum would be show-

ing up any time now, from work. From the bank.

But at the same time the girl could not banish from her mind's eye that bulging black quilt on her mother's bed, and the terrible white face of the constable who'd seen what was under there.

SEVEN

A Woman's Touch

Gosfield was a claustrophobic side street whose chief attribute was not having been blown up in the war, as yet; a row of nondescript brick apartment buildings faced another, exchanging what struck Agatha as glaring expressions, as if each were slightly miffed its opposite would dare stand so close. Margaret Lowe's flat was just around the corner from an intersection where a fish-and-chip stall and several pubs provided this dreary working-class neighborhood with fried nourishment and alcoholic relief.

The late afternoon was bleakly overcast, evening impatiently crowding in, with light, half-hearted snowfall, making intermittent appearances; it was just chilly enough to be a bother.

Agatha had worked a full day at the hospital, having requested that tomorrow, Friday, be free, so she could be unencumbered to prepare for and attend an event to which she looked forward almost as much as she dreaded it: the premiere of her new play.

She'd just been trading her white lab coat for her Glen Plaid, when Sir Bernard had leaned into the dispensary and said, "We have another. Would you like to accompany me? . . . I must warn you, my dear, I'm told our friend has outdone himself."

She had of course accepted the invitation, and by now had become blithely blasé about the breakneck Spilsbury style of motoring, though James, in her lap, did seem rather alarmed, the terrier a seasoned passenger who usually insisted on sticking his head out the window. At the moment James's snout was buried in her bosom.

On the way, Agatha posed a question she had been meaning to ask the pathologist for some time.

"These women," she said. "How long does it take them to die at the strangler's hands?"

"There's a variable . . . and it would be no different for a man, suffering that fate."

"And what is the variable?"

"Whether the victim is breathing in when the murderer's grip tightens, squeezing off the air . . . or breathing out, at that moment."

"What does the variable amount to?"

"Thirty seconds, if one happened to be breathing out—breathing in, fifteen."

"Not terribly long."

"No, my dear—terribly long indeed. It would seem, I should think, even at fifteen seconds . . . interminable."

Sir Bernard parked behind Inspector Greeno's

Austin—although truth be told, the inspector could have walked to the crime scene, so close was it to his recently established special headquarters at the police station on nearby Tottenham Court Road. James waited in the Armstrong-Siddeley; an animal would hardly be welcome at a crime scene.

And that thought had barely passed through Agatha's mind when an attractive teenaged girl exited the door up to the flat, with her arms filled by a Scottie terrier. Closed in behind the window of the parked sedan, James began to bark furiously, and the other terrier enthusiastically responded to the call of the wild.

The teenaged girl—whose expression, Agatha thought, might best be described as "shell-shocked"—hugged the dog close to her. A uniformed policewoman, who had exited the building just behind the girl-and-dog, was at the child's side now, guiding her by the arm, speaking to her softly, the words drowned out by the pair of yapping animals. With James muffled behind the rolled-up car window, his barks seemed echoes of the other terrier's.

Agatha paused, watching the policewoman escort the girl—a dark-haired, long-stemmed budding beauty—into the front passenger seat of a waiting police car.

Sir Bernard—as usual, minus a topcoat, in an impeccably tailored black suit with red carnation—was at the door to the stairwell, holding it open with one hand, the oversize Gladstone bag in the other. He looked at her anxiously, almost cross. "Agatha . . . ?"

"That must be the dead woman's child," she said, hollowly.

"Most likely," Sir Bernard said.

He had told her the basics of the affair on the ride over : the teenaged girl, home for a long weekend, her knocking unanswered, going to a neighbor, who fetched a bobby.

Agatha fell in line, Sir Bernard leading the way up a narrow poorly illuminated flight; this was hardly a "ladies first" situation.

The girl had instantly brought to mind the image of Agatha's own daughter at that age, who had been similarly beautiful (and still was). Agatha could only hope this young woman was as free-spirited and independent as her Rosalind. Though she knew her love for Rosalind was reciprocated, the mother felt sure that, when the day came, her daughter would not suffer the terrible emotional upheaval Agatha had suffered at the loss of her beloved Clara.

Three doors shared the landing, where Inspector Greeno and a uniformed constable waited. The center door was closed—the common loo, no doubt; the door at the right was filled by a harshly attractive blonde who looked thirty-odd but likely was still in her twenties.

The inspector was interviewing the woman, who stood in her doorway smoking a cigarette; she wore an improbably virginal white-and-pink floral housedress and her rather startling hair was in pin curls. This probable prostitute seemed genuinely sorrowful, and was clearly cooperating with the inspector without the sexual fencing in which Ivy Poole, at the previous crime scene, had indulged.

Inspector Greeno said, "Miss Wick, my pathologist and secretary have arrived . . . if you'll excuse me."

"Shall I wait inside my flat, 'spector?"

"No, I'll be with you again, shortly."

The landing was getting crowded and the inspector sent the constable down to street level, to keep any interested citizens, and particularly the press, away.

The third door, the one at left, was open, revealing the flat within, which, while a single room, took up a fairly large area, though perhaps the sparseness of the furnishings furthered that impression.

A single bed was against the facing wall, on which a black eiderdown covered a protuberance that likely was the victim's corpse. On a small table at the head of the bed was a porcelain pitcher and basin and a few towels. On the floor, at the foot of the bed, a scattering of female apparel included a green cloth coat with a rabbit-fur collar, a navy jumper, a frilly white blouse, a chemise, and a little blue pillbox hat with a gay red feather.

For such a frightful, seedy flat, these were surprisingly nice clothes, Agatha noted. Of course, they were the woman's working garb. The spider, not the web, attracted, after all; but what terrible sort of fly had been summoned?

Depending on where one stood on the landing, the rest of the scantily furnished flat could be ascertained, for the most part. At the left was a small kitchen area with a table and counter with open shelving below with a few pots and pans; on the counter was a hot plate and a few stacked dishes and cups, but no cupboards above and no sink. At the right, a sitting area with two straight-back chairs faced a small fireplace. The wooden floor had two drab threadbare rugs, one in the kitchen area, the other under the bed.

The tawdry little flat was more striking in what it hadn't than in what it had: no bureau, no wardrobe, no sink with running water, no icebox. *Where did she keep her clothes?* Agatha wondered. Then she noticed the suitcases under the bed.

Inspector Greeno was saying to Sir Bernard, "I'm afraid I left the comforter in place, Doctor. Under no circumstances did I want to subject the victim's daughter to the sight of her mother."

"Who identified the deceased?"

From her doorway, Miss Wick chimed, "I did, dearie. He left her face alone, small favor."

"Otherwise," the inspector continued, "the constable did a nice job of not disturbing things. You certainly won't find a shortage of evidence. The fiend used every damn thing he could lay hands on, on the poor wench. . . . Pardon my bluntness, ladies."

"Not at all," Miss Wick said, from her doorway.

Agatha said to the inspector, "Is there any doubt that this is the same assailant?"

But it was Sir Bernard who answered, "There's always doubt. We make no assumptions before we've examined the evidence. . . . Ready for me in there, Inspector?"

"Photographers haven't been here yet, Doctor. I wouldn't remove anything, just yet."

"Understood."

And Sir Bernard and his massive medical bag of tricks entered the bleak flat. Carefully stepping around various items on the carpet near the bed, and avoiding the piled clothing, he knelt, opened the Gladstone bag wide, and withdrew his rubber gloves. He rose, put on the gloves like a surgeon preparing to operate, and was lifting the eiderdown gently off the corpse when Inspector Greeno stepped in front of Agatha and pulled the door shut to the flat.

Agatha looked with undisguised irritation at the inspector, but Greeno's narrowed eyes and a gesture of the head indicated to her that this action was taken due to the presence of Miss Wick, and not herself.

Softly, almost whispering, the inspector said, "I'll not deny you entry, Agatha, when Sir Bernard has completed his examination of the victim and the various evidence."

"Thank you, Ted."

"But I beg you to carefully consider whether you need expose yourself to such unpleasantness."

"We've had this conversation before, Ted."

"I know we have, Agatha. And I believe my respect for you has been made clear." He nodded toward the closed door. "But that's the work of a sexually deranged, homicidal maniac, in there. They pay me to have nightmares. You needn't volunteer for this misery."

Genuinely moved by his concern, Agatha touched the man's sleeve. "Thank you, Ted. But I'm a big girl."

A loud voice, nearby, interrupted the sotto voce conversation. "Excuse me, but I work evenings. If you don't need me, 'spector, I could stand to get on with me life."

Miss Wick's sorrow had abated sufficiently for her to become annoyed by the inconvenience, it would seem.

"I do have a few questions," the inspector said, turning to the attractive if harshly made-up blonde.

Both Inspector Greeno and Agatha took notes as the former asked several questions. Miss Wick again was cooperative and businesslike.

"The daughter didn't know her mum was a working girl," the woman said. "And I think Pearl turned to it, late in life . . . at least, late in hers, right?"

"I'm not sure I follow," the inspector admitted.

"Well, she was a respectable woman, a landlady at a seaside boardinghouse. But the army come and evicted her—took over her place for barracks and such."

Agatha had a shock of recognition—she'd been similarly "evicted."

"She was a right good-looking woman, for her age," Miss Wick said.

"How old was she?"

"In her cups one night, she admitted to bein' forty-two. It says something about her, you know, favorable like, that at her age the men would still seek her favors."

The fifty-odd Agatha decided not take offense. Young women in this profession lived hard and died young. Age, it would seem, was relative.

"You called her 'Pearl.' "

"Yes. Her daughter calls her 'Margaret,' but it's Pearl, on the street. Calls herself Pearl Campbell, or she did, anyway. That's the name you'll find on your books."

"She's been arrested?"

"Last week, you fellas was 'round 'cause of a row she was havin' with a soldier. Right noisy, it was."

The inspector exchanged glances with Agatha, saying to Miss Wick, "Who called to complain?"

"Well . . ." Suddenly Miss Wick seemed embarrassed. "I denied it, when she accused me . . . I told her it musta been them in the flat, other side of hers . . . but it was me, all right."

"That's . . . not exactly according to your profession's code, is it?"

"I would never turn no girl in for making a few honest bob. Dishonest, maybe you'd call it. But I had a gentleman caller meself, at the time, and the noise got so bad, my guest got nervous and flew the coop."

"I see."

"Besides, maybe he'da hurt her or somethin', the bloody row goin' on over there. So I was doin' her a favor, really, callin' it in—wouldn't you say, Guv'ner?"

"Did the police come?"

"Yes—like I said, it'll be on your books. Ask the bobby on this beat—he's right downstairs!"

"I'll do that."

"They wrote the soldier up, too. Good-looking boy."

"RAF?" the inspector asked, possibly because of Cadet Cummins, Agatha supposed.

"No. Canadian. Nice boys, the Canucks; but they don't spend as free as the Yanks."

"Was there any noise last night? Or this morning?"

"No. And I didn't see Pearl at all last night. No idea who she was entertainin'. . . . It's the Ripper, ain't it?"

"You did your friend a favor. Allow me to do you one."

"What's that?"

"I won't take you in on suspicion of soliciting, if you agree not to go out tonight."

She frowned. "Don't nick me, Guv. I got but one date tonight and he's a regular. No harm done."

"Miss Wick, you live and work in the middle of this monster's stamping grounds. You stay in, till we get him."

"Is that advice or a threat?"

"It's advice. The threat is down on the street. . . . You identified the body, didn't you?"

"I did."

"Do I need to say more?"

"No, Guv."

"Thank you, Miss Wick. You go on inside, now. There's a good girl."

And she did.

"Will she listen to you?" Agatha asked.

"No. But she'll stay with her regular clients."

"The murderer might be a regular client."

The inspector grunted a humorless laugh. "Precisely. One credible theory regarding the original Ripper had it that Jack was a habitue of prostitutes who caught a disease from one and took his rage out on many."

"You'll check on this Canadian soldier, of course."

"Of course." He sighed mightily. "Solving a murder is like doing a jigsaw—all you need do is fit the pieces together . . . but you have to find them first."

She shook her head in admiration. "What you do, Ted, requires incredible patience."

"It does at that. Real policework is careful plodding, questioning, screening, sifting. Before tonight, our Ripper hadn't left us many clues."

"But now he has?"

"He may have. Sir Bernard will tell us. You'll note at once that the fiend's madness, his . . . blood lust, if you'll forgive the melodrama . . ."

She smiled gently. "Melodrama is my business, Ted."

He returned the smile, though his seemed weary. "Well, he's accelerating in viciousness."

"As did the original Ripper. Perhaps our man is a kind of 'copycat,' too."

"I think he well may be. But these mutilations reveal a loss of control, not the execution of some master plan. You'll see a small armory of makeshift weapons, in there—each potentially a carrier of fingerprints and other clues."

When finally Sir Bernard allowed her to enter, he stayed in the doorway, watching her. Because the photographers had not yet arrived, the pathologist had not collected any of the evidence, merely made his observations.

The late Margaret Lowe lay stiff and naked on the cheap cotton-covered divan, which was heavily, darkly stained with blood. Despite her condition, it was clear she had been a striking woman with a fine figure, very much the beauty her teenaged daughter would one day be.

Agatha prayed the daughter's fate would be kinder.

The victim's eyes were open wide and pink with burst blood vessels, her mouth open in a silent scream;

around her neck a much-darned nylon stocking had been tightly knotted.

Thirty seconds to die, Agatha thought. *She was screaming when she went . . . breathing out, then.*

The mutilations were as promised—a shocking escalation of the previous murder: razor slashes on the breasts and stomach, and the lower part of her body stabbed and slashed, again and again. As a terrible final gesture, a candle had been employed in an obscene fashion.

She turned away with a shudder. Eyes lowered, she saw the "small armory" on the rug: a bread knife, a carving knife, a razor blade, a fireplace poker . . . all bloodstained.

A hand touched her arm and she started.

"I'm sorry, Agatha," Sir Bernard said. "I thought . . ."

"I'm not feeling sick . . . just sick at heart."

"I know. The objectivity of your medical training must come to bear."

"Is this the world, Bernard? Is this the world we live in now?"

"Only a part of it, Agatha."

"Evil . . . so evil."

Watching as she went, so as not to disturb any evidence, she moved away from both Sir Bernard and the bed, pausing in the small sitting area by the fireplace. Her eyes went to the mantelpiece, where stood a cheap chrome-plated candlestick.

She moved closer, raising a finger like a child wondering if a burner should be touched. "Bernard . . . this is where he got the candle . . ."

"Very probably."

"You can see the fingerprints!" She wheeled, excited. "You can see all kinds of fingerprints."

Sir Bernard, whose focus had been on the corpse and the area surrounding, came to have a close look. "Cherrill will have a fine time with this," he said, smiling tightly as he leaned in, keen-eyed.

Then the pathologist frowned.

"What is it, Bernard?"

"These are fingerprints from a *right* hand. . . ."

She took a closer look, herself. He was correct. But then she smiled. "Yes, but when a left-handed person removes a candle from a candlestick, he holds the candlestick with his *right* hand . . ."

Sir Bernard's eyes sparked. "And grasps the candle in his left! . . . Very nice, Agatha. Very nice indeed."

A voice behind them said, "Excuse me—Sir Bernard, I'm not sure what we should do about this. . . ."

"About what, Inspector?"

Inspector Greeno looked almost as pale as the corpse. "I just got word from a motorcyle dispatch rider." He held up the message in his hand. "We have *another* one. . . ."

One of Inspector Greeno's detectives, arriving with the police photographer, took charge at the Margaret Lowe crime scene. Superintendent Fred Cherrill himself had been called to take over, and to collect the fingerprints.

Sir Bernard, with Agatha and her terrier in tow, followed Inspector Greeno to Sussex Gardens, Paddington— in the same Edgware Road district as Montague Place, where the Hamilton woman had been killed. With the inspector in the lead, Sir Bernard could not careen wildly through the blacked-out streets of West London, for which Agatha was grateful (James, too).

The ground floor flat consisted of two rooms—a kitchen and a bedroom. Unlike Margaret Lowe's spartan quarters, these were fully furnished digs, with modern kitchen appliances and the bedroom well and comfortably furnished, judging by the glimpse Agatha received before Sir Bernard closed himself off in there with the corpse of Doris Jouannet.

The flat, while nice enough and palatial in comparison to their last stop, did not speak well of its late tenant's housekeeping habits. On the kitchen table were dirty dishes, and in the nearby sink another stack of the same. A layer of dust that would have petrified Hercule Poirot provided an unpleasant patina throughout.

The inspector and Agatha were seated at this squalid kitchen table with the devastated husband of the murdered woman, who had been a willowy blonde of thirty-two.

Henri Jouannet was seventy-four. Slender, with light blue eyes setting off a narrow face that had been handsome some decades ago, he wore a neat dark-gray suit and a lighter gray tie, and was a well-groomed old gentleman, but for the occasional stray hairs growing out of his ears and nose.

The constable who'd met them outside told the inspector that Doris Jouannet was known in the neighborhood to be a "good-time girl," a part-time prostitute who seemed to have been in the game for thrills as much as extra money.

Her husband appeared unaware of this. He had taken

British citizenship ten years ago. Presently he was night manager at the Royal Court Hotel in Sloane Square, Chelsea. This explained his spiffy dress, in the midst of this squalor, Agatha knew: the Royal Court was a reasonably fashionable hotel.

The old fellow sat at the table, slumped and in shock, but responding to the inspector's questions. Talking helped keep his wife alive, for just a little while longer.

"I sleep here," the hotelier said in his musical French accent, "only on my night off—t'night, T'ursday. Other night, I sleep at the Royal Court, you know."

The inspector asked, "When did you see your wife last?"

"Yesterday. We eat together, every night. Last night, she cook the meal, we eat at this table. Then she accompany me to the station, Paddington Station. She say to me, 'Good night, Henri,' very sweet. Her last words to me were, 'Don't be late tomorrow, my darling.' "

He covered his face and wept quietly. Agatha offered Mr. Jouannet a handkerchief from her purse, and he accepted gratefully.

"*Merci.*" He shook his head. "Who could do such a terrible t'ing?"

The inspector did not reply, instead saying, "I know you've been over this, sir, but please tell me what happened this evening. From the beginning, if you would."

Mr. Jouannet nodded, swallowing, drying his eyes with the hanky. "I return to the flat not long ago . . . hour ago, maybe. I am surprised to see the milk bottle, it was not taken in. I go in to the flat and I shout out, 'Doris!' But there is no reply. And the supper things from last night, they are still on the table. This is not like my wife. She is a good wife, you know, good housekeeper."

Agatha could hardly agree—the layer of dust in this apartment had taken longer than overnight to accumulate. But she of course said nothing; the old man's high opinion of his late wife's housekeeping abilities seemed the least of his illusions about her.

"I was worry, and see the bedroom, it is locked, and now I know something, something is . . . what is the word? Amiss. Something is very amiss! I could get no reply, for my knocking and my shouting, so I go to the building manager, and we send for the police."

"Neither you nor the manager had a key to the bedroom."

"No! Well, I have a key, I tried the key, but it did not work. For some reason, unknown to me, my Doris, she put a new lock on the bedroom door."

He wept again, but talked through it, describing the arrival of a pair of constables, one of whom had broken down the door while the other held the husband back.

"The bobby, he come out, and he look pale, like the bottle of milk. He say, 'Sir, don't go in, sir,' and then he tell me . . . my wife. She is dead."

He sat forward now, leaning on both elbows, covering his face with his hands and Agatha's handkerchief. She rose and stood next to him and placed a hand on his shoulder, squeezing from time to time.

Finally, Inspector Greeno said, "Mr. Jouannet—do you have any reason to think there would be another man in your flat last night?"

"No! None at all. We have been happy, these six years. Some, they say the age difference, it would be . . . difficult. But no. We are in love."

"I see." Inspector Greeno shifted in his chair. "I'm going to request that you return to your quarters at the hotel, sir. We'll need to do some work here, and you really need to sleep elsewhere, tonight."

"I don't want to leave her!"

Agatha said, softly, "Mr. Jouannet . . . your wife is not here. She's with God now. You must get some rest."

He swallowed and looked up at her. "You are very kind. I will have your handkerchief laundered and return."

"Please, no." She patted his shoulder. "The inspector can arrange to have you driven back to your hotel."

And that was done for the old fellow.

Then Agatha and Inspector Greeno were seated at the filthy kitchen table, alone but for a pair of uniformed men milling out on the landing.

"As if this weren't horror enough," Agatha said, "that poor man will soon learn from the tabloids that his wife had a secret life."

The inspector sighed. "They were both working the night shift, all right. Damned shame."

Sir Bernard appeared in the bedroom doorway, his hands in the rubber gloves, his expression typically grave. He made a small motion to Inspector Greeno, who rose and went to him. Though the invitation may not have included her, Agatha rose as well and fell in alongside the inspector.

Sir Bernard shook his head. "We have a madman on

parade, here, no question. But looking at the wounds . . . and judging by the wounds I examined at the Lowe flat . . . he's definitely a left-handed madman."

The inspector nodded. "When was she killed, do you think?"

"The body's still warm."

Agatha said, "The Lowe woman was last night's victim. Mrs. Jouannet is tonight's."

"I think you're right," the inspector said. "He's on a spree—one killing a night. But why in hell did he *miss* a night?"

"Perhaps," Agatha said, "we should merely be grateful he hasn't attempted to make that one up."

Sir Bernard said, "We should get Fred Cherrill over here to do the fingerprinting personally, when he's finished at the other crime scene."

"Agreed," the inspector said.

"May I enter?" Agatha asked.

Sir Bernard said, "Really, my dear, it's just more of the same savagery. . . ."

"Though not so redundant," Agatha said firmly, "as to discourage you from spending half an hour with her. . . . I have an idea I wish to pursue. It may prove helpful."

The two men exchanged glances, obviously curious what this helpful idea might be.

So, once again, she was allowed to examine the crime scene, and—since, as before, the police photographer had not been around to do his job yet—she took special care neither to touch nor disturb anything.

On a chair at the foot of the bed the woman's clothes were heaped. On the dressing table lay a bloody safety razor blade—on the carpeted floor, an open, rifled handbag minus any money.

Doris Jouannet had been a slim, fair-haired woman, reasonably attractive. She lay sprawled across the double bed, clad only in a flimsy light blue dressing gown, which apparently had been ripped open by the frenzied killer. The bedclothes were disarrayed, and perhaps this time a brief struggle had preceded the inevitable.

Again, a knotted silk stocking was tightly knotted around the victim's neck. From the expression on the dead woman's face, Agatha felt this had been a fifteen-second death—one small, unintentional mercy. Though the killer had lacked a "small armory" this time, and had been confined to the use of a razor blade, the slashing to breasts, stomach and the sexual area were shockingly deep, and resembled the Lowe woman's mutilations.

Agatha spent little time studying the corpse, however; that was better left to Sir Bernard and his forensics expertise.

But she felt sure Dr. Spilsbury's focus had been again entirely on the body, and she brought her own feminine skills and instincts to bear as she looked around the dust-covered room that the late Mrs. Jouannet had bequeathed to the investigators.

She had an idea that the bequest would be a generous one . . .

. . . and she was correct.

On the dressing table was a hand mirror, on which fingerprints could be detected by the naked eye. This, however, was not as interesting to Agatha as the cleaner, distinctly formed patches on the table's dusty surface.

Several objects had been removed from the table, obviously—possibly by the killer, who was, after all, a thief.

She summoned the two men and pointed out her discovery.

"That shape indicates, I would say," Agatha mused, "a fountain pen. Or some other similarly shaped object. And this I would say is just big enough to be a pocket-comb, minus some teeth. This, a wristwatch."

An edge of excitement in his controlled voice, Sir Bernard said, "We need photographs of these. And measurements."

The inspector was smiling, nodding. "The photographer will be here momentarily; I'll do the measurements myself." He turned to the mystery writer. "Agatha, your woman's touch may make a real difference, here. . . ."

"It's the lack of a woman's touch," she said, gesturing to the dusty dressing-table top, "that made the difference."

February 13, 1942

Four murders in five days.

All had been committed within two miles of Piccadilly Circus; but nighttime revelers did not abandon the West End.

The United States military responded to the Ripper threat by expanding the number of their own police on the streets—snowdrops, the MPs were called, thanks to their distinctive white helmets, floating visibly above crowds in darkened Piccadilly.

The tabloids were irresponsibly fueling the notion that the Ripper was an American soldier, and all over town mothers were telling their young daughters to beware of American soldiers, all of whom were rapists. In the meantime, the flowers of the night continued to bloom around the Americans and their superior pay. Some were neither streetwalkers nor call girls, rather

factory workers and even precocious school girls, looking to milk an escort for all he could give and then slip
away into the night.

Not that all of the Americans were as naive as com-
monly thought: they dismissed British films as stodgy
and boring; hated the beer; weren't impressed by the
dance halls; and missed being able to drive, even if on
the wrong side of the street.

They did, however, like the women—deemed them
hospitable, and not as sophisticated as they'd been
warned.

There were those—Americans and Londoners alike—
who considered the city in the blackout, particularly in
winter, a thing of beauty, with a fresh tang in the air.
Whatever the season, the Americans found London fra-
grant—a city with no central heating, burning cannel
coal, that oily form of shale leaving its distinctive pun-
gent odor behind. Even to locals, the city did smell surprisingly good—petrol fumes were largely gone, with so
few vehicles on the streets. (Horse-drawn wagons had
increased, with their own attendant fragrance.)

London in the moonlight could reveal the architec-
tural wonders of classically constructed buildings;
lovers—whether an engaged couple or a temporary al-
liance—might walk hand in hand along the moonlight-
shimmering Thames or down a cozy side street to enjoy
the blackout's romantic calm ... or was it a lull? A
moon could light a bomber's way, after all. ...

The Blackout Ripper—the press continued to hammer that designation home—did not love the moonlight;
he was shielded by darkness, killing in silence, targeting

women of the street, though a respectable lady out alone, like Margaret Hamilton, might be mistaken for his chosen prey.

If the good-time factory and school girls momentarily outnumbered the street-hardened prostitutes on the West End, it was because the latter understood they were the preferred victims, and were too scared to venture out, knowing that the streets they usually haunted were haunted by another predator who utterly out-classed them. He would strike again, the new Ripper, that seemed certain—the lust of killing had him in its malicious grip.

Jack the Ripper murdered his eight or more victims over a period of well over a year.

But even Jack the Ripper had never murdered four women in five days.

EIGHT

Survivors

The woman across the desk from Inspector Ted Greeno in his small temporary office at Tottenham Court Road Police Station sat with her shapely stained-tan legs crossed and her arms folded over her considerable bosom.

Ten years ago, the features of her heart-shaped face would have rivaled any budding film actress; but now, at perhaps thirty-five, those features had hardened into a kind of mask, emphasized of course by her heavy make-up, from her phony beauty mark to the scarlet gash of her generous mouth; in the harsh light of the station house, the caked make-up was obvious and settled unflatteringly in pockmarked patches along her rouged cheeks. Her dark blue eyes were hooded and her light blonde hair was due not to a bottle but her own nordic heritage, and for all her hardness, it was not difficult for Ted Greeno to understand why a mug might part with a few bob for her favors.

"You don't believe me, do you, Guv?"

"A thousand pounds would see you pretty, Greta, for a good long time."

One of the tabloids, *The News of the World*, had posted a thousand-pound reward for "information leading to the capture, arrest and conviction of the Blackout Ripper." This had brought the doxies out of the woodwork, and Greeno was using four men in as many interview chambers to thin out the hordes of suddenly cooperative ladies of the evening.

Greta's story had been interesting enough to bring her to the attention of the inspector himself.

She claimed that last night—about two hours after the latest victim, Doris Jouannet, had been slain—a young airman had approached her at the bar at the Trocadero. He struck up a conversation with her and bought her a drink and a sandwich. According to Greta, the airman flashed a wad of Treasury notes her way and made "an indecent suggestion." When she declined this offer, and left to walk toward her apartment, he followed her and shoved her into a doorway and said, "At least let me kiss you good night," and when she said no, he began to strangle her.

"I struggled with 'im, kicked him in the family jewels, and he dropped something . . . his gas-respirator, I think . . . and I screamed bloody murder and he went runnin' off, into the darkness, like a scared rat."

That was the story that Greeno was now reflecting upon. Finally he said to her, "How can I believe your story, Greta, when it's riddled with lies?"

"Did I do this to meself, then?" Greta Heywood asked, opening her pink silk blouse a button and indignantly gesturing to her bruises on her throat.

"No, but your ponce might have done."

"I don't work with no bleeding ponce!" she blurted. "I'm a one-woman business, I am."

This was an interesting outburst for two reasons.

First, Greta had hitherto clearly avoided copping to any solicitation of prostitution with the phantom airman, weaving an incredible story of her "virtue" being challenged.

Second, she had inadvertently led Greeno to a relevant realization: none of the working girls attacked, at least those who'd taken the Ripper to their flats, had fallen under the protection of a procurer, or "ponce," as girls like Greta called them. In many cases, a ponce would have been watching from a distance (perhaps with cosh in hand to help liberate the mark of his loot). In other instances, a ponce might share the flat, lurking in an adjacent room or behind a blanket draped on a clothesline as a partition.

So the Ripper had either been careful to avoid the procurers, or had been damned lucky.

"Greta, you'll not be charged with soliciting. Tell me what really happened."

"Well . . . it's just what I said, or mostly was. I met this RAF bloke at the Troc. I already had a date I was waiting for, but this one was cute. So I told the bloke he could have a quickie, if he liked. So after we had a drink, we saunter across to that side street . . . by the Captain's Table?"

Greeno nodded. "Go on."

"I was leading the way with me torch. I snapped it off and we stepped in a doorway and he started in makin' love to me. Kissing me. I don't let just any steamer do such a personal thing as that . . ."

A steamer was a client, a mug—cockney rhyming slang: steamtug, mug.

". . . but he was a pretty boy. Kind of sweet and shy . . ."

Could she be telling the truth? That might have been young Cummins she was describing.

". . . sweet and shy, that is, till he started chokin' me to death! Gor blimey, did I let him have it in the—"

"The rest of your story is substantially true, then."

"'Course it is. What kind of girl do you take me for, Guv?"

Greeno allowed that one to slide past. Then he asked, "Did he really drop his respirator?"

"Swear on me mum's grave, he did. I heard the clunk."

"All right. I'm going to send you over to the Trocadero with my sergeant. You show him how and where this all occurred."

The inspector put this in motion, then returned to the desk in the cluttered little office, where he lighted up one of his trademark cigars. A map of Central London with pins in the murder spots covered most of one wall, filing cabinets huddled along the other, and he sat facing a glass-and-wood wall looking out on the bullpen of constables and detectives as well as the receiving desk.

It did sound like Cummins. The other flier in the case, that Canadian, the one who had argued with Margaret Lowe, was in the clear: he had shipped out the day after Miss Wick phoned in her noise complaint.

But Cummins was the only one of the St. James Theatre suspects who had an ironclad alibi for the murders of Evelyn Hamilton, Evelyn Oatley, Margaret Lowe and Doris Jouannet: the cadet was in billets when each murder was committed! The billet passbook proved the times he came and went, and his roommates backed the passbook.

And why, of all the airmen in London, should it be Cummins, anyway? The St. James Theatre was linked only to one of the crimes. Allowing Agatha Christie Mallowan to participate in this investigation had Greeno thinking like a bloody book writer, not the hard-nosed cop he was.

Agatha's detectives could gather a tidy group of suspects in the library to discuss the clues and reveal the villain, who would politely go along with the process, right down to presenting his hands for the cuffs. The reality of real policework, and Ted Greeno's life, was that his only avenue of inquiry at the moment was a seemingly endless parade of streetwalkers. He had spoken with a hundred girls (some five hundred had passed through these portals), sometimes for a few minutes, other times (as with Greta) for a considerable spell.

And having to depend on the unreliable likes of Greta for his leads did not give Greeno a good feeling— these girls were, after all, liars by trade, even without a tabloid offering a thousand pounds for the right story.

The telephone shook him shrilly from this cynical reverie; and in his ear was the deceptively soothing baritone of Superintendent Fred Cherrill, the finger-print expert.

"I support Mrs. Christie's observations about the fin-gerprints on the candlestick from the Lowe flat mantel-piece," Cherrill said. "A right-handed person, in snatching the candle from the candlestick, would natu-rally place his left hand on the base, using his right to grasp the candle. The process would be reversed in the case of a left-handed person."

She had bleeding Cherrill thinking like a thriller writer now!

"Actually, Fred," Greeno said, between cigar puffs, "she prefers 'Mrs. Mallowan.' But she has a keen eye, under any name."

"Indeed. Those impressions in the dresser-top dust at the Jouannet flat may prove valuable. But so far the fin-gerprints from the Lowe flat aren't, terribly."

"Why is that? Smudged again?"

"No, they were beauties—textbook examples of the art; in addition to the candlestick, perfect prints showed up on the half-finished glass of beer, and on a hand mir-ror. We just don't have any corresponding prints in our files."

"How is it possible that a vicious wrong 'un like our Ripper doesn't have a previous criminal record?"

"Well, he doesn't. Perhaps he's a late bloomer. Or an American G.I., like they say. But when you do find a good suspect, Ted, we'll have excellent prints to check him against. Any other leads?"

"Nothing from the Jouannet place, beyond what Mrs.

Mallowan spotted. Oh, I did find a broad roll of Elasto-plast in the drawer of that same dresser."

"Sticking plaster, hmmm. Anything significant about it?"

"Probably not. But the adhesive tape had a small ob-long piece cut out of it, recently I would say. If it was used to patch one of the stolen items . . . well, hope springs eternal."

"As does despair. Incidentally, no good fingerprints at the Jouannet pigsty—and I gathered and processed them personally, on the scene."

Greeno grunted. "Well, fingerprints or not, it was clearly the same man. These killings are quite specific in their savagery."

"They are indeed—Spilsbury confirms the slashing and strangulation indicates a left-handed murderer, just as my fingerprint evidence does. We are, it would seem, close."

"And yet so far," Greeno said, dryly. "Thanks, Fred."

"Cheerio, Ted."

Of the stories from the prostitutes, the most com-pelling concerned the urbane civilian client who called himself variously the Duke and the Count, whose smoothness disappeared when the actual sex came into play. He was rough. Some of the women claimed he "strangled" them during the act . . . as one wilted flower put it, "Playful-like, y'know?"

Greeno was working double-shifts, so he'd had to de-cline Agatha's generous offer of tickets to the opening night of her new play. The actors would be on the boards

by now, he thought—it was mid-evening, after blackout—and he hoped his friend was enjoying herself, and
that her fictional murders were being well-received.
These thoughts, somewhat ironically, preceded the first
real break of the case.

Phyllis O'Dwyer—the prostitute whose friends
spoke of an encounter between Phyllis and a "wild"
customer who may have tried to kill her—finally turned
up, under her own steam.

Thirty-odd, another attractive woman whose features
had hardened into soulless near-immobility, Phyllis
O'Dwyer sat with her shapely silk-stockinged legs
crossed as she smoked, blowing occasional rings. Her
eyes were light blue and wide-set, another heart-shaped
face with a fake beauty mark; her hair was a shade of red
unknown to God but familiar to West End beauty shops.
She wore a black suit with a startling red silk blouse, and
was the kind of cheap that could prove expensive.

"You've been looking for me, I hear," she said. She had
a ragged voice, having suffered too much drink, too much
screaming, over the years . . . possibly too much drunken
screaming. "I wasn't hidin' or nothin'. Couldn't this
bleedin' big police department find one little redhead?"

Phyllis was five-eight and weighed a well-shaped ten
stone, easily.

"It's amazing," Greeno admitted, lighting up a
fresh cigar, "what turns up, when a thousand pounds is
involved."

Her eyes flashed. "I ain't here to lie, Guv. I had the
life scared out of me, ain't ashamed to say. Crikey, I
thought I was a goner, sure."

Rocking back in his swivel chair, arms folded, Greeno said, "Why don't you tell me your story, Phyllis."

"No call for that attitude, Guv. I come in here of my own free will, a good citizen doin' you a good turn. No call for you callin' me a liar."

"I never did."

"I can read between the lines. I'm a lot of things, but a fool ain't one of them. I tell you, Inspector, it's true, every blessed word of it. And if you don't believe me, you can stick my story right in your . . . files."

"Go on, Phyllis. My ears are open and so is my mind."

"Cor. Well. You plan to charge me two pounds for this?"

She meant was Greeno going to nick her for prostitution, if she copped to that; two pounds was the standard fine for solicitation.

"No. It's a free ride."

She smiled with casual laciviousness. "No free rides in my trade, Guv. . . . Anyway, here you have it. I meet this airman outside Oddenino's restaurant in Regent Street. Cadet, he was."

"How do you know?"

"He was wearin' a cadet's white flash. Are you going to interrupt me, every whip stitch?"

"No."

"So I take him home, see, and it was cold as hell, and my little flat was chilly, even with the gas fire, so I kept on a pair of boots. Some blokes like that anyway, it's a bit of a kink, isn't it? Also, just for show, I left on a necklace I'm partial to. Stones set off me eyes."

Risking Phyllis's wrath, Greeno asked, "What sort of necklace?"

"Big old thing. Costume jewelry. If them jewels was real, I wouldn't be makin' my livin' on me back, would I now?"

That seemed to be more or less a rhetorical question, so Greeno merely nodded politely.

She was saying, "So he says to me, 'Do you always wear a necklace in bed?' He was lyin' next to me. We'd already . . . done the deed. Sort of turning the center stone around in his fingers, like. And I say, 'Sometimes. Some blokes like a little glamour.' And I kinda kicked a foot in the air, showin' off me boot. It was a joke. But I don't think he liked it none, 'cause he grabbed hold of the necklace and started to twist it . . . you can see the bruisin' on me neck."

"I can."

"So he's got a whole handful of the necklace and was twistin' it like mad. I was choking, bleedin' chokin', I tell you. And his eyes . . . kinda blue, they was, funny shade . . . they was blazing. Just like a madman's."

"How did you survive it, Phyllis?"

"Damn near didn't. I was in agony. I was swearin' at him, when I could spit anything out at all—and fightin' to get the necklace loose off me throat . . . and in me bleeding death throes, I lash out my feet! God bless them boots. If I didn't have them on, I . . . well, I think I got in a lucky kick, I must have done, turnabout's fair play cause he had me jewels and I got him in his, and he screamed like a ninny, and fell off the bed, arse over teakettle."

"What did you do then, Phyllis?"

"I yanked the necklace off and I say, 'Hey, what the bloody hell's up with you, Tarzan?' I was breathin' hard and wonderin' what he would do next . . . but he was down on the floor, all quiet-like all of a sudden. Breathin' hard his own self. Almost like he was cryin'. Very quiet, he says, 'I'm sorry. Very sorry. I get carried away sometimes.' I say, 'I'll carry you away to hell and gone!' And he stands, and he's diggin' in his pockets . . . he already give me five pounds. Now he gives me another fiver, to show how sorry he was. I snatched it from him and told him to get the hell out. And he did."

Greeno studied her. Her eyes were wide and bright and the recollection of fear was palpable in her manner. She was not, in his view, lying.

She began to dig in her little purse, and soon she came up with two crumpled fivers. "I stuck the notes away in a drawer. Didn't spend 'em."

"Why not, Phyllis?"

"I thought . . . with all this Ripper stuff in the papers, maybe they would be clues. You could trace 'em, like."

Tracing banknotes was always difficult, but as Greeno examined these, he noticed that they were two in a series, which would make matters much easier.

"When did this happen, Phyllis?"

"Tuesday night. Not long after dark."

That meant the Ripper likely had an unsuccessful go before he'd finally hooked up with Nita Ward.

"Could you recognize him in an identification parade?"

"Like he was bloomin' Churchill."

The O'Dwyer woman refused to be taken into protective custody—"If you blokes couldn't find me, not bloody likely that madman could do"—but left Greeno with a contact telephone number.

Greeno sat in his office, in a blue cloud of self-created cigar smoke, smiling to himself, which was a relative rarity in this case.

He believed her. Phyllis O'Dwyer had survived the madman's attack—she could identify the bastard. This was their first real break. . . .

The second one came about fifteen minutes later, in the form of the plainclothes sergeant who had accompanied Greta Heywood to the Trocadero for a reconstruction of the attack she claimed to have survived.

The sergeant, a hard-eyed round-faced veteran of the vice detail, held up a gas mask.

"It was right where the girl said he dropped it," the sergeant said. "Kind of out of sight, Guv, behind a trash bin."

Greeno reached across the desk and took the respirator; the masks had always struck him as otherworldly-looking things, straight out of H. G. Wells. The mask's goggle eyes stared at him briefly, before the inspector turned the thing over and saw a beautiful row of numbers: 525987 . . .

. . . an airman's service number.

They could trace him now.

Two living witnesses.

They had him. Whether this was Cummins, or one of the thousands of other RAF fliers . . . they had him.

The question now was, could they stop him before he made it five murders in six nights?

NINE

Smashing Success

For Agatha, first nights were misery.

She attended the dreaded events for two reasons and two reasons only.

First, after weeks of rehearsal and the building of sets and the gathering of props and costumes and the efforts of so many . . . the time had finally come; and the poor actors had to go through with it, didn't they? And she, as the author, felt it only fair to share their misfortune, should things go awry. She was, after all, the instigator of the crime; and one should pay for one's crimes.

On the opening night of *Alibi*, for example, the script enjoined the forcing open of a door to reveal a murder victim; but the door had jumped its cue and swung open prematurely, revealing said victim in the act of lowering himself to the floor. Such agonies (and the anticipation thereof) were heightened on first nights and the play-wright felt a responsibility to share the torture with her accomplices.

The second reason was far less noble: the thing that killed the cat . . . curiosity.

Even though she had attended a number of re-hearsals, Agatha had only a disjointed sense of the play as performed. Even attending a dress rehearsal—which she had not, in this instance, sitting instead with Inspec-tor Greeno at the Golden Lion, for the interviews that had followed Nita Ward's murder—did not give an au-thor the full sense of a play.

An audience was required for that—an audience who might laugh in the right or wrong places, an audience who might respond well or in a lukewarm manner or even in sheer walk-out-of-the-damned-thing hostility.

Right now she was just one of that audience, seated un-obtrusively to one side, about ten rows from the orchestra. Aware of eyes upon her, and of murmurs of recognition ("There she is," "That's her"), she sat quietly with her in-vited guests on her either side—Sir Bernard Spilsbury and Stephen Glanville—waiting for the lights to go down, to provide her with the anonymity she so craved.

Such sentiments considered, she was not quite sure why she adored the theater so, why in her heart of hearts she preferred the role of playwright to that of novelist. In her youth, before she had developed this miserable, horrible shyness, she had performed in plays and given piano and vocal recitals without a care. Perhaps now, in her self-conscious adulthood, she was performing through the actors, personal appearance by proxy.

Or perhaps it had to do with her propensity for living in a world of fantasy, at the center of a self-created, interior stage suited for drama, comedy and her own particular brand of melodrama. She'd had imaginary friends as a child, and even now she heard her characters speak within her and often merely felt the recording secretary of their thoughts and discourse.

She had been accused, by reviewers, of using dialogue as a sort of crutch, of short-changing the art of narrative by leaning so heavily on what the characters said to each other. This technique, she'd been lectured, was simplistic.

Her only defense was the work itself—that publishers and readers accepted this approach. To her, dialogue was the engine of a story, and perhaps she was not a novelist at all; perhaps she was a dramatist who occasionally staged her productions within the covers of a book.

Tonight, however, the play would be staged at the St. James Theatre, and she must endure all of the attention and fol-de-rol attendant with any opening night. The after-party would be held at the Savoy, and the procession of Rolls Royces that would carry "celebrities" such as herself and the director and producer to the theater began there, as well.

(The publicity-averse Sir Bernard had chosen not to participate in this indignity, and arranged to meet her later at the theater; he'd even offered to give Stephen a lift, and Agatha savored with pixie-ish glee the thought of cool and collected Professor Glanville being subjected to a wild ride with the Mr. Toad who was Sir Bernard Spilsbury.)

A West End opening, like everything else in war-time, required adjustments. The play would begin at seven p.m., not eight, and the caravan of celebrities had begun at six, prior to nightfall and the blackout. This al-lowed the event to include flash photographers and an illuminated marquee and a general emulation of the giddy hysteria of a pre-war premiere, even though the bombed-out remains of Willis Sale Rooms next door, and the ravaged Christie's Auction House across the way, provided stark reminders of reality.

Often scavengers, poor things, were seen digging through the rubble of these buildings, the once-grand Willis in particular. The bobbies had no doubt chased any such unfortunates away, before the red carpet and velvet ropes were put in place at the St. James; the war-zone reminders of the Willis site and Christie's across the street could not be banished, but the ragtag home-less, the war refugees of London, could be chased away, temporarily, at least.

Agatha, sharing her Rolls with Larry Sullivan, frowned at this bitter irony—again, she could only won-der if the homicidal frivolities she dispensed had any place in this war-torn world.

A surprising crowd awaited them, held back by con-stables, and timidly she smiled and waved at the blur of people who shouted, "Agatha! Agatha!" at her, as if she were a film star; oddly, the real star of stage and screen at her side, portly Francis L. Sullivan (looking rather like a head waiter in his evening dress), received fewer of these complimentary catcalls than she.

Certainly Agatha did not feel like a film star. She felt

like an overweight middle-aged woman, rather embar-
rassingly stuffed into a navy chiffon pleated evening
gown that had been purchased several seasons (and two
stone) ago. Her fur coat, however, hid a multitude of
sins, and the passage down the red carpet and into the
lobby was blessedly brief.

The lobby was closed off to the public, and a small
cocktail-party-style gathering of the principals—ex-
cluding the actors, of course, who like brides before the
wedding must not be seen—was under way, the night's
nervous participants milling about sharing best wishes
(including the quaint American admonishment that they
should all "break a leg") and shaking hands and kissing
cheeks and calling each other "darling."

She sensed a chilliness, however, from several of
those who had participated in the recent interrogation at
the public house next door.

The cold front had first moved in at the Savoy when
Larry Sullivan barely spoke to her. In the backseat of
the Rolls Royce, she asked her actor friend if he was
miffed with her.

"Miffed?" the portly actor asked, arching an eyebrow. "That hardly states it. How, Agatha, could you
participate in that inquisition?"

"If you mean Inspector Greeno's questioning, I
thought it was polite and perfunctory. Really, Larry,
we'd all come in contact with a victim in the most notorious murder case of the war. Police queries were
inevitable."

He huffed. "Surely you don't suspect me of indiscre-
tions."

So that was it: Larry was not worried that he might be considered a murder suspect, but that his lovely bride, Danae, might hear tales out of school.

"Of course not," Agatha assured him. "I really don't believe the inspector has his eye on the St. James bunch at all, at this stage."

"You mean, because of the other two killings."

"That's right. This seems a murder spree, clearly, and any thought that the Ward girl was someone's murdered mistress has fallen by the roadside."

Larry's eyes popped. "Is that what the inspector thought?"

She touched the black sleeve of his tuxedo. "Larry, please. The inspector doesn't think anything. Let's save the melodramatics for the stage, shall we?"

Embarrassed, Larry rode in silence for a while, then turned to her with a child's little smile. "I would just hate for you to have a bad opinion of me, Agatha. I think the world of you."

"I'm sure you do, darling," she'd said.

The coldest of them was probably Irene Helier Morris. The actress-turned-director had traded in her mannish rehearsal togs for a lovely black gown that showed off a figure that managed to be willowy and curvaceous at once. Her make-up was perfection, her dark blue eyes highlighted beautifully, her lipstick a bold crimson.

"I'm surprised you didn't bring your inspector along," Irene said, with a chilly smile.

"I asked him," Agatha said, realizing the woman had

been trifling with her, "but this loathsome case has him working evenings."

In a rather premature display of celebration—the curtain had yet to go up, after all—waiters in red jackets threaded through the little party with silver trays of champagne-in-glasses. Irene plucked one off. Agatha did not—she did not indulge in alcoholic beverages.

"If I didn't know you better," Irene said, "I'd think you pulled us into this wretched affair for the publicity."

"You do know me better."

"Well, there hasn't been any press, it's true. Don't think I haven't considered it myself—plays in this climate can use any boost they can get."

Not sure whether the director was trifling or not this time, Agatha smiled her most winning smile and said, "If you do turn this into a publicity stunt, my dear, neither you nor your husband need approach me again about producing one of my plays. . . . Excuse me."

"Agatha," the director said, touching Agatha's shoulder—she had already turned away, "forgive me. Opening night jitters."

Agatha turned and cast a sincere smile at the woman. "I understand. Do know that I think you've done a lovely job."

"It's a wonderful entertainment. I don't believe I could have mucked it up if I'd tried."

Now Agatha gave the director a smile to wonder about. "Oh, I'm sure you could have done, darling."

Leaving Irene with a confused frown, Agatha found Janet Cummins and her cadet husband Gordon standing rather awkwardly against a wall—obviously feeling the outsiders. He was a most handsome boy in his blue uniform, and Janet was a knockout, proving the truth behind the cliche of a secretary turned raving beauty by taking off her eyeglasses. Janet's full-bosomed figure was well-served by a pink off-the-shoulder gown.

"Well, Airman Cummins," Agatha said and offered her hand.

He took it and half-smiled. "I'm afraid I don't know whether to shake this or kiss it."

"Entirely your choice."

He shook it and all three of them laughed lightly.

"You are ravishing," Agatha told Janet. "You belong up on that stage."

The. producer's secretary beamed and all but blushed. Her complexion was peaches-and-cream and her brunette hair was nicely curled. The thought that Airman Cummins would have any need to go trolling among streetwalkers, with this pretty, voluptuous wife at hand, struck Agatha as absurd.

"I'm afraid," Janet said, in belated response to Agatha's compliment, "that my childhood ambitions to be an actress were quashed by a terrible strain of stage fright."

"I suffer the same malady," Agatha admitted. To the RAF cadet, she said, "I'm so delighted you could get leave for this evening."

"Actually, I had picket duty again, but your friend Stephen Glanville, at the Air Ministry, arranged it for me. I have the whole night off to spend with Janet, don't have to report in till nine a.m. He's a true gentleman, Mr. Glanville is."

"He is indeed. He'll be here tonight. I'm expecting him momentarily."

"I feel a fool, Mrs. Mallowan," the cadet said, "not bringing a book for you to sign."

"Did you forget?"

"Well . . . I thought it might be bad form, considering the occasion."

"Nonsense. I'll fix you up at a later date."

His grin was infectiously boyish. "I'm so anxious to see how you've made this one into a play. The book ended so . . . finally."

"I warned you before, young man—I've changed the ending. I hope you won't be disappointed. Perhaps you can give me an honest appraisal, after the performance."

"If I like it," he said, "I'll gush with praise."

"And if you don't?"

He shrugged. "I'll gush with praise."

They all laughed again and Agatha excused herself, to respond to Bertie Morris. The round producer with the matinee idol's face stood off to one side, motioning at her frantically.

She joined him and said, "Why the semaphores, Bertie?"

"I need a favor. The critic from the *Times* desires the briefest of interviews."

"Well, then, here it is: no."

"But Agatha . . ."

"No. And if, at curtain, you try to 'surprise' me by

requesting that I respond to the 'author, author' outcries with a speech, I will refuse . . . perhaps not graciously."

"Not a speech . . . just a few words. . . ."

"Bertie, must we have this conversation again? I cannot make speeches. I never make speeches. I won't make speeches."

"But Agatha . . ."

"And it is a very good thing that I don't make speeches, because I should be so very bad at them."

Bertie's expression of disappointment melted into a warm smile. "Well, I had to try, didn't I, darling?"

She returned the smile. "I suppose you did."

"You've written a simply wonderful play."

"I would settle for 'good.' "

The producer chuckled, but the warmth in his eyes seemed genuine. "Agatha, in your quiet way, you are the most difficult prima donna of them all."

"Bertie, you alone of the people I have called 'darling' tonight truly are . . . 'darling,' that is. And thank you."

"Whatever for?"

"Well, for producing my play, for one thing, and selecting your lovely talented wife to direct, for another, as well as assembling such a fine cast in wartime. But also for being the only participant in those Golden Lion interviews, the other day, who hasn't chastised me."

"Oh, that! I thought it was exciting. A police inspector asking questions about a murder—rather like one of your plays!"

He seized a glass of champagne from a passing tray and moved on.

Twenty minutes later, Agatha was sitting in her inconspicuous seat off to one side between her two extremely handsome escorts—Stephen Glanville and Sir Bernard Spilsbury.

"Did you enjoy the ride?" she whispered to Stephen.

His eyes widened, and he whispered back: "I'll have my revenge one day, my dear. . . . Didn't you invite our inspector friend?"

"You're the second person to ask me that. He's working on the murders even as we speak."

Stephen's expression grew serious. "It still troubles me, you in the midst of that grotesque Grand Guignol. Tell me, are you having nightmares?"

"Not at all," she lied. Well, sort of lied: the murder scenes had not turned up in her dreams; but the Gunman of her childhood nightmares had been with her every night this week.

She turned to Sir Bernard. "Thank you for accepting my invitation."

"I had to miss a concert for this, you know," he told her with a sideways glance that seemed vaguely reproving.

Agatha touched her bosom. "Oh, dear no . . ."

"Yes. It's on the BBC this evening."

And he smiled a little.

She chuckled. Those who considered Sir Bernard an aloof stuffed shirt didn't know him very well.

"I feel privileged," he was saying, "to accompany the author to a first night. And as possibly the only human being in the British Empire who has not yet enjoyed one of your thrillers, I look forward to the experience."

Moved, she took Sir Bernard's hand and squeezed it in thanks.

Stephen looked past Agatha to say to the pathologist, "A word of advice, Sir Bernard—if you figure out the mystery, don't tell her. Annoys the bloody hell out of her."

Agatha said, "Stephen," sharply, but was amused.

Also, he was right. Max had figured out the novel tonight's play was based upon, and she had never forgiven him.

The lights dimmed, and an expectant audience burst into applause. Bertie Morris came out on stage into the spotlight to welcome the first-night audience and Agatha did not hear a word of his speech, which wasn't very long. She was nervous, as if about to go on stage herself.

But she needn't have been. The performance—by a splendid cast that included Henrietta Watson, Linden Travers, Percy Walsh, Terence de Marney, Allan Jeayes, Eric Cowley and Gwyn Nichols—was letter perfect; no corpses were up and around (at least no unscripted corpses) and the audience tittered and even laughed at her occasional dark humor, gasping in collective fright and surprise at all the appropriate moments.

She was pleased. She liked the play and admired what Bertie and Irene had done with it. And the audience applauded long and loud, Agatha losing count of the curtain calls. At the end Bertie came out and introduced Irene, who bowed and spoke briefly; to the cries of "author, author," Bertie gestured to Agatha in the audience and—reluctantly, terribly embarrassed—she stood and took a little bow.

The audience rose to its feet—her first standing ovation! How wonderful; and the applause ringing off the rafters was sheer music.

And Bertie, God bless him, had done no more than introduce her in the audience—no attempt to shame her into a dreaded speech.

When the lights came up, she did stand in the aisle and speak to a number of audience members, and consented to sign programs, novels and autograph books. She did not mind speaking, briefly, one person to another, with an intelligent fan. And anyone who liked her work qualified as that. Around such friendly, ordinary people as these theater patrons, her self-consciousness and nervousness were blissfully absent.

For that reason she became the last of the celebrity guests who would be chauffeured by Rolls Royce to the Savoy. Even the actors were able to remove their makeup and trade their costumes for evening wear before Agatha had finished tending to her adoring public ("Best you've written, dearie!" "First class—thumbs up, I'd say!" "V-signs for this one!" "Loved every minute!").

The caravan of Rolls Royces had to make several trips, and Agatha waited in the theater lobby, away from the glass doors, for her ride to come. The fuss, thankfully, was over. The street outside the theater was empty but for Janet Cummins and her cadet; Janet had been assigned to look after Agatha, as the rest went on, Rolls by Rolls, to the party in a private room at the Savoy.

Only a handful of theater employees remained— even the ushers were gone; an assistant manager was tending to matters in the box-office booth. While she

waited for her ride, she strolled back into the theater.
The curtain was up, revealing the set of a lavish modern
living room with balcony windows looking out on a
painted sea.

A question had been answered for her tonight.

She had witnessed and heard the response of a wartime audience to her play, which was one of her most particularly bloodthirsty—seven murders and a suicide. And
they had loved it—every blessed ghoulish minute of it.

These were terrible times indeed—from the atrocities
of the war itself to the current spate of West End sex murders in which she'd allowed herself to become embroiled.

And never had the escapist fare she served up been
more gratefully received, like much needed nourishment.
When the post-war world came, she would fit in just fine.
She might make the books a little deeper, psychologi-
cally, to cater to a public not so innocent, as in golden
days; and, thanks to her experiences with Inspector
Greeno and Sir Bernard, she would take pains to make the
police and legal procedures more accurate and realistic.

But other than that, the "sausage factory" (as she
thought of herself) would stay in business, thank you
very much.

Feeling as though a weight had been lifted from her
shoulders, she walked back into the lobby and the explosion shook the building like a giant cannonball and
threw her to the slanting floor, where she in her furs and
finery went rolling into a corner between the box office
and the stairwell, as the entire lobby caved in, the
sounds of it beyond deafening, an avalanche of building

materials raining down, sending up clouds of dust and powder.

Someone screamed—not Agatha; a woman on the street, probably Janet Cummins. Dazed, ears ringing, Agatha pulled into the corner even more, as the ceiling continued to pour down in unceremonious chunks, stirring pulverized brick and stone and mortar into cloud upon filthy cloud.

Then—a settling. . . .

She took stock of herself, and her situation.

She could not stand—a portion of the ceiling slanted across, caught against the side of the box office, forming a little room four feet by five. She was covered in the filthy aftermath of the explosion, but did not seem to be injured. Using her nurse's knowledge, she checked herself carefully, as the caved-in lobby continued to settle itself with groans and grating.

Perhaps her ankle was sprained.

Nothing more seemed wrong. She'd been flung to the floor and she'd rolled to a stop, but no bones were broken and she had suffered no concussion. Breathing was difficult, with the dust-filled air, and she covered her face with a handkerchief from the pocket of her fur coat, which had itself helped cushion her fall.

So in that sense she'd been lucky.

She could hear voices beyond the fallen slabs and wreckage of the former lobby, but could not make them out. No air-raid siren had preceded the blast, nor was one now cutting the night—*that* she would hear, despite the blockage.

If not an air raid, what could have happened?

And then, as she knotted the handkerchief around her face like a bandit, she remembered the rubble next door that had been the lavish Willis Sale Rooms, a favorite spot of scavengers and looters. Perhaps they had made an unintended discovery: an unexploded bomb.

That would explain her current situation.

She glanced overhead and saw that slanting slab, the remnant of the former roof that was her current ceiling, and it seemed to be shifting, ever so slightly, creaking like the ancient hinges of a door in a haunted-house film, spitting pebbles and grit.

Beneath the handkerchief, she smiled bitterly.

And so it had come to this: Agatha Christie (not Mallowan), the originator of so much mayhem, caught like a mouse in a trap, waiting for the ceiling to fall in and kill her.

What a terrible thing it was, possessing a heightened sense of irony: the only thing in all the world that truly frightened her was the thought of being buried alive. She had avoided the air-raid shelters for this very reason, staying in bed with a pillow over her face.

Well, she had no pillow here, did she? But she would remain calm. She would not give in to this phobia. She would not become a silly hysterical old woman.

Examining the pile of rubble before her, roughly parallel to where the street would be, she got on her hands and knees and, still in her fur coat, began to dig her way out. She had no trouble for a while, feeling good about the effort.

But then that slab ceiling shifted and dropped and she let out a little scream.

The wall and other debris caught the slab, preventing it from squashing her, but that "ceiling" was only a few angled inches above her head, now. She was in a coffin. Buried alive. A Poe-like death for Agatha Christie. . . .

Praying (not for herself, for Max and Rosalind and any grandchildren who might one day be born), she kept at it, pawing at the rubble, clearing the way of little pieces, bigger pieces, and was making progress until she reached a larger block of sideways ceiling, not unlike the slab overhead. She could not get a grip on it; and had she been able to have done, she would not have had the strength to move the thing. . . .

Breathing heavily under the handkerchief now, she slumped and exhaustion seductively whispered in her ear, fatigue stroking her every muscle, bone and sinew: rest. Sleep. Wait. Someone will come . . .

. . . death, perhaps.

And the impasse before her, the slab of ceiling, moved, as if of its own accord.

She could hear the grunt of a manful effort being made, and then that slab slid away, and for just a moment she had a glimpse of a face—the young cadet!— and the street . . .

. . . and then more detritus rained down and filled the opening.

But between the two of them, Agatha and her cadet

savior, the way was cleared; another slab of ceiling provided shelter from the fragments above, making a passageway, and she reached out her arms to the boy and he grasped her hands and pulled her, ever so gently and yet firmly, through the aperture.

He helped her to her feet, saying, "Mrs. Mallowan, dear God, are you all right?"

She hugged the cadet and smiled into those boyish handsome features and said, "I have never been better . . . thanks to you, young man."

A sudden lurching sound behind them, a crunching and crashing of shifting wreckage, drew their immediate startled attention: the passageway through which Agatha had escaped no longer existed.

But she did.

She touched the boy's cheek and whispered, "Thank you, my dear."

He lowered his eyes, chagrined. "My motive was selfish—I couldn't abide the thought of this world without your books."

The street was filled now, with spectators and constables and a banshee scream that was not an air-raid siren, rather the announcement of the impending arrival of firemen.

Janet Cummins was fussing over the rescued writer, and helping Agatha brush herself off; there was something comical, farcical about standing in a fur coat and evening gown, layered with powdery filth. The air out here was breathable, but also suffused with a dirty haze; the voices of the constables were raised, attempting to secure order.

Agatha, remarkably clearheaded, said, "Was anyone else in the theater? Wasn't someone in the box office?"

"That was Clemens," Janet said, "the assistant manager. He was in his office, locking the money box in the safe. He was unaffected by the explosion—the lobby took the full force of the blast. He was able to get out a side exit."

"A UXB, probably," Agatha said. "Some poor scavenger went to heaven in a hurry, I daresay."

And at that moment, finally, her ride came, the Rolls Royce rolling up grandly. The liveried chauffeur emerged wide-eyed as Agatha approached.

"I am perfectly all right," she said, "but I wish to be examined at University College Hospital. You will drive me there."

The chauffeur said, "Yes, ma'am," and held the rear door open for her.

Janet and her cadet helped Agatha into the backseat of the Rolls.

"We'll go with you," Janet said, leaning in, eyes wide with concern.

"Don't be a silly goose. Take a taxi to the Savoy and report that any rumors of my demise are bound to be at least slightly exaggerated. . . . Young man . . . Gordon, isn't it?"

The cadet leaned in next to his wife. "Yes, ma'am."

"You remind me so of my first husband. He was a handsome hero, too. How ever can I repay you?"

Covered in filth, the boy's smile was as white as the rest of him wasn't. "A signed book would be more than sufficient."

"Give me your address, then. Write it down."

Frowning, Janet said, "That can wait. You're dazed, Mrs. Mallowan."

"No," she said. "I will take care of this as soon as I'm home, which will be tonight, if I have anything to say about it. Any special title, Gordon?"

He had found a play program somewhere and was jotting down his address with a pencil. "This is at the receiving center, Mrs. Mallowan. Where I'm billeted. . . . I could use the new Poirot, if you have an extra."

"*Evil Under the Sun,*" she said, and smiled.

She reached out for the program, but the smiling airman was still writing.

With his left hand.

TEN

Suitable for Framing

In that most undignified of garments—a hospital gown—Agatha lay between the crisp white sheets of a crankable bed in a small temporary room off the emergency ward.

Over the past hour and a half or so, she had been thoroughly examined, poked, prodded and probed, and had passed with flying colors, though her left ankle had been wrapped in service of that minor sprain. A concerned doctor, whom she knew well from the course of her pharmacy duties, suggested that she be admitted overnight for observation; it was, however, her decision . . . this the doctor made clear. She declined.

It was just past midnight, the presumed end of a long, memorable and exhausting day; but Agatha felt strangely alert, her thoughts clear, her energy high. Nearly dying had been a most exhilarating experience. There would be precious little sleeping, tonight.

Further, she had—in her state of clarity in the little chamber off the emergency ward—assembled in her mind the pieces of the real-life series of murders, in much the manner she applied to the creation of her fictional crimes. Real life seemed at once simpler and more complex than her concoctions. . . .

Inspector Greeno wondered why the killer's spree had been interrupted—why no killing Wednesday? The answer was painfully simple: Cadet Airman Gordon Cummins had fire picket duty that night; he could not get out, Wednesday night, to have his nasty fun.

And, though it was theoretical (albeit an informed opinion), Agatha knew exactly how Cummins might have got around the billet book, which might explain as well the apparent false evidence of the roommates who had vouched for him.

She hoped she was wrong.

Her evidence was circumstantial at best; and she was at war with herself over her conclusion. *How could that sweet boy who had saved her life be a sex-crazed murderer?* He had written for her directions to his billet using his left hand, and what of that? Was every left-handed man in London a suspect, then?

In all probability, the fingerprints found at the two murder scenes yesterday would provide conclusive confirmation (or exoneration) of the cadet, once the great Fred Cherrill had processed them. Sir Bernard's forensics examinations would further either indict or clear. She need do nothing but relax either here in a cozy hospital bed or at home in her own comfortable flat, waiting for the police to do their job. She was not, after all, Jane Marple, much less Hercule Poirot. And even Poirot had sense enough to allow the likes of Inspector Japp to take the physical risks.

And yet she had to know. The thing that killed the cat was nibbling at her. The puzzle-piecing portion of her mind craved the boy's guilt; and the sentimental side of a woman whose life had been valiantly saved provided a yearning for his innocence.

Thankfully, no one from the St. James crowd had come calling. She had sent strict orders with the chauffeur to convey to the after-theater party at the Savoy that she was fine but wished under no circumstances to be disturbed tonight; she needed her rest (a lie) and they could come calling tomorrow, if they liked, when she was home again.

Quite likely the director and producer and others on the production staff were at this very moment huddled in a back private room of the posh hotel, oblivious to the hors d'oeuvres (though probably not the cocktails), wondering whatever to do—the play appeared to be a hit, judging by the enthusiastic response of the audience, and she herself had seen the *Times* critic walking out with a smile on his usually merciless lips. But with the theater damaged by that apparent UXB, the play and its players were as homeless as the poor rabble who'd unwittingly set off that bomb.

She had requested a robe, and this—a green flannel affair—is what she wore as she slipped out of the emergency ward and headed for the upper floor area that was home to the Department of Pharmacology and the dispensary. Rather absurdly, she had thrown her fur coat over the robe and hospital gown—after patting the fur free of as many little dirt and dust clouds as possible— but she abandoned the torn and filthy navy evening gown, thankful that she would never again have to force herself into the wretched thing.

Her keys to the pharmacy were in her purse, which lay somewhere under a ton or so of rubble where the St. James lobby had been. Her plan of action had been to find a member of the hospital janitorial staff to unlock the door for her, but no need: a charwoman was at work.

She exchanged pleasantries with the charwoman, who asked, "Where's your pup tonight, missus?"

"Home asleep," Agatha said cheerily, "dreaming of chasing rabbits across the commons, no doubt."

The charwoman said, "He's a good 'un, James is!" and returned to her sweeping, without apparent notice of Agatha's bizarre wardrobe. In a small room off the pharmacy (itself cramped quarters), Agatha went to her locker, which—despite its name—was never locked.

This was where Agatha, upon arriving to work, would hang her Burbery and change into her lab coat; but she also kept a spare blouse and skirt—should there be any unexpected spillage in the dispensary—and a pair of sensible shoes and fresh pair of stockings, black woolen, knee-high. Since she was, at the moment, barefoot, the latter items came particularly in handy.

On the top shelf of the locker were three of her author's copies of the new Poirot novel; she kept these within reach, as now and then a co-worker or patient would talk her out of one.

A single copy of *Evil Under the Sun* tucked under an arm, she left the dispensary, more or less dressed—the fur coat over white blouse and dark gray skirt—and, as she had expected, light glowed behind the pebbled glass of Sir Bernard's laboratory.

She peeked in to the specimen-lined, bottle-and-beaker flung cubbyhole. "Working all hours again?"

Looking very much like Sherlock Holmes, Sir Bernard, in his lab coat, sat perched on a stool at the counter with a microscope before him; but in one hand was a big-eyed Halloween-worthy gas mask, which he was examining through a magnifying glass held in the other.

He looked up sharply and his words were edged as well. "Whatever are you doing out of bed, young lady? I was just about to come down and check on your status."

She moved to his side; a small pile of what appeared to be sand rested on a slide that had as yet to be slid under the microscope. "I have a clean bill of health, I'll have you know. . . . I was hoping for a ride home, but you look to be in the midst of things. What do you have there?"

He held up the bug-eyed mask. "Inspector Greeno had it delivered around—it's a gas respirator, part of an RAF kit. A man who may be our Ripper dropped it when a potential victim proved uncooperative."

Another black mark against the boy; could young Cummins be so careless, so stupid? She began to wonder if this accumulation of clues was too good to be true—was there a possibility the cadet could have been fitted for a frame?

Frowning, she asked, "When did this happen?"

"Last night, I believe. That is, Thursday night. It is now technically Saturday." Having delivered this typically precise pronouncement, the pathologist held the magnifying glass over the surface of the mask for her to look; she did so and saw nothing of note.

But the pathologist did: "I've found something most interesting on the fabric."

"And what would that be?" she asked, since he seemed to want her to do so.

"Sand! I'm about to compare it to sand and mortar fragments taken from the air-raid shelter where the Hamilton woman's body was discovered."

She frowned thoughtfully. "Can that gas mask be traced?"

"Most certainly—there's an Air Force number stamped inside. I spoke to the inspector . . . he's working 'round the clock, it seems . . . and he's getting in contact with your friend Glanville, to put the number with a name."

She risked a smile. "Playing with sand is a far cry from performing autopsies, Bernard."

"Agatha, forensics only begins with medicine. Science is science. . . . May I make a suggestion?"

"Always."

"Why don't you borrow my Armstrong-Siddeley? I can take the train home, when the time comes."

"That's very kind of you. I hope it wouldn't be too much of an imposition. . . ."

"Nonsense." Then he looked at her. "This assumes you are in a condition to drive." He arched an eyebrow and only one who knew him well could have detected the trace of a smile. "I would hate for anything to happen to my Armstrong-Siddeley."

She grinned her most unguarded, horsey grin. "I know, Bernard. You're so careful with it." She gestured elaborately to herself. "No concussions, no broken bones. Tiny sprain—my left ankle. Otherwise I'm fine."

"And you would like to go home and get some rest in your own bed? Understandable."

She left with the keys to Sir Bernard's automobile, the great man wholly unaware that she had entered his lab with that very intention.

Agatha prided herself a lay master of psychology. She felt certain her friend would have come to the hospital in order to keep an eye on her, and would pass the time by going to work on something or other in his laboratory.

And once Sir Bernard had become involved with his work, he would be loathe to leave it, not even to give his ailing friend a ride home from the hospital. . . .

Agatha had her own agenda, and driving to Hampstead to the Lawn Road Flats to curl up in bed was not first on that list.

It should have been: this she knew. Now that the gas mask had turned up, with its identifiable service number, the guilt or innocence of Cadet Cummins would soon be ascertained by Inspector Greeno and his minions. No need for any further involvement on her part; she was a civilian observer who, common sense would say, needed to retreat to the sidelines, and promptly.

Later she would reflect upon the events, and wonder if she would have behaved so recklessly, had the earlier brush with death not taken place. For now, she merely moved forward following her intentions.

St. John's Wood had changed, since the time she and her first husband had lived there. In 1918, when Agatha and Archie had first moved to London, the district had been one of big old-fashioned houses with large gardens. Now the area had been invaded by large blocks of drearily modern flats, taking the place of many of those homes, particularly the smaller ones.

The address Cummins had given Agatha took her to Viceroy Court, between Edgmont and Townshend Streets, a particularly large example of the lusterless modern buildings that had invaded the district, a seven-story structure faced with yellow brick. Requisitioned for billets by the RAF, the building could not have dated back more than a few years and had a cold institutional quality that displeased Agatha.

Having left the Armstrong-Siddeley on the street, Agatha—a most unmilitary figure in her fur coat, copy of the new Poirot tucked under one arm—approached the building, which loomed monolithically in the moonlight. She entered to find the lobby a functional area of the same yellow brick with a few patriotic posters on several bulletin boards—"Let's Go! Wings for Victory," "Tell Nobody—Not Even Her!" and (irony again, she thought) "Hitler Will Send No Warning—Always Carry Your Gas Mask."

A pair of guards in RAF uniform played cards at a small table near the door; looking painfully young to her, they looked up at Agatha curiously. Standing, one asked, "Help you, ma'am?"

"Just visiting my nephew," she said.

"At this hour, ma'am?"

"I only just got in to town by motor—terrible delays. He said he'd be up late. Am I breaking a rule? After visitors' hours, is it?"

"We don't stand on ceremony around here, least not on the weekend. What's his name, ma'am?"

"Gordon Cummins."

"Oh," the guard said with a smile. "The Count!"

Oh dear, she thought.

"Pardon?" she said.

"Nothing, ma'am, just a sort of nickname the blokes call your nephew. . . . I'm not sure LAC Cummins is in, ma'am. Hardly anybody is, y'know. Friday night. It's an empty building, you've dropped by to."

"I spoke to him on the telephone. I think he's expecting me."

"Do you know what billet, ma'am?"

"I do indeed. Room 405."

"Go on up, ma'am."

The guards returned to their cards—that new game, gin rummy, if she wasn't mistaken—and took the automatic lift to the fourth floor.

Flats faced each other across a central hall, in hotel fashion; the brick walls and the tile flooring again gave off an institutional air which seemed appropriate for the building's commandeered use as a billets, but which must have been depressing for apartment living.

The guards were correct: the hallway was deserted. No Saturday night parties or card games could be discerned, no radios blared behind doors. The troops had no doubt descended upon Piccadilly.

She hoped she wouldn't have to return to the lobby to request that one of those young guards unlock Cummins's door for her—and she didn't: after her knock went unheeded, she tried the knob and found it unlocked. Not surprising, in what was after all a glorified barracks.

The flat, drably modern, was a sitting room beyond which lay a small, separate kitchen and two small bedrooms, one of which was off the kitchen, the other off the sitting room, which also had an adjacent bathroom. Four cots had been erected in the sitting room and each cramped bedroom had a single cot. Those using the sitting room were apparently living out of small wooden RAF-issue trunks; but each tiny bedroom, glorified closets really, had bureaus—Viceroy Court had apparently provided furnished apartments to its prior tenants.

The small bedroom off the kitchen—with its easy access to the fire escape—was Cadet Cummins's, or so she assumed. The reason for her deduction provided one more small irony: on the bureau were two stacks of popular inexpensive editions of her novels.

That much, at least, had been true: Gordon Cummins was a fan, a dedicated reader of hers.

She did not even have to open the drawers of the bureau to find what she'd been looking for: near one stack of her books, beside multiple sideways displays of her own name, were the apparent souvenirs of slaughter: a cheap comb missing teeth; a fountain pen; and a woman's wristwatch.

Though it would take measurements and the forensics skills of Sir Bernard to confirm so, Agatha's eyes told her these items mirrored the shapes she'd discovered in the dust at the Jouannet murder flat.

Leaning closer, narrowing her eyes, she thought she could make out something odd about that watch: it had something on the back of it. . . .

She lifted the cheap watch and turned it over and saw the oddly cut piece of elastic tape, fitted there for the original (late) wearer's comfort, again seeming to mirror the shape of the portion cut from the roll of sticking plaster Ted Greeno had found in a drawer of that dust-covered dresser in the Jouannet place.

Finally, an inexpensive silver-plated cigarette case, bearing the initials N.W., seemed to indicate the ghost of actress Nita Ward. A pack rat, this killer was; not a good thing to be, in that line of interest.

"What a pleasant surprise . . . "

Startled, she turned to see the owner, or at least the possessor, of these ghoulish keepsakes: the boyishly handsome RAF cadet, Gordon Cummins, standing with cap in hand, his smile sideways, his eyes a greenish unblinking blue.

And in a flash she recognized him, finally: the Gunman.

The smiling blue-eyed Gunman of her childhood nightmares, who had come back to haunt . . . and perhaps warn . . . her in recent nights.

How like Archie he was.

"Oh, do forgive me," Agatha said, turning her back to the bureau and beaming at her host. "I was driving home from the hospital, and I simply couldn't sleep, and thought I'd run over and leave this here, to surprise you. . . ."

She held out the copy of *Evil Under the Sun* for him to see, then placed it on the bureau top behind her.

"I still need to sign it, I'm afraid, but I wanted to thank you properly. I thought you were spending the night with Mrs. Cummins."

He shut the door. The cadet remained near the door, but the bedroom was so small, so claustrophobic, that they still stood relatively close to one another.

"I thought when you got back," she said, "that you would find the book in your bedroom and just be . . . pleasantly surprised. But then, you said you were pleasantly surprised, just now, didn't you? And I hope that's true."

He said nothing. Still smiling. Twisting the hat around in his hands.

"Well . . . perhaps I should go," she said. "I'm afraid I was misguided . . . invading your sanctum sanctorum, as I have."

"No," he said. "I'm pleased to see you. . . . The party broke up early. Everyone was too concerned about you, and the explosion at the theater, for the merriment to continue."

"Ah."

"Janet was upset, and suggested I go on back to my billet. No night for celebrating, really. . . . Do you suspect me?"

The bluntness of that struck her like a blow, but she did her best not to show it, saying quickly, "No. But I'm afraid the police do."

He sat on the side of the bed, which hugged the wall lengthwise, opposite the bureau; his unblinking eyes stared into nothing. "But I'm innocent. I hope you believe me."

"Oh, I do, Gordon. You're my savior, after all. My knight."

His eyes met hers and his smile turned into a crinkly thing, as if unsure whether or not to become a frown. "If they caught him . . . this Ripper . . . he wouldn't be as famous as the other one, would he?"

"I'm afraid I don't understand."

"Well, the first one . . . Jack . . . they never caught him. He was too smart for them, they'll say. But the truth is, he didn't have Sir Bernard Spilsbury and these modern detectives up against him, did he? Fingerprints and things."

"No. He didn't. It was all quite crude then."

"But if the new Jack were to kill someone famous, that would be different."

"I'm afraid . . . afraid I don't follow you, Gordon."

He shrugged, the smile boyish as ever, charming. "Well, imagine if the Ripper killed you, Mrs. Mallowan. Mrs. Christie. What headlines that would make—the fiend who killed the mistress of murder. That would make history."

"I suppose so. If you were guilty. But I don't believe that you are."

His eyes tightened and, finally, he blinked. "You don't?"

She sat next to him on the bed and patted his hand reassuringly. "Certainly not. You're a smart boy, Gordon. Would a smart boy like you leave such obvious clues just scattered about? These things on your bureau. . . . worthless items, a toothless comb, a fountain pen, a cheap watch."

He was frowning in thought. "Then you see it, don't you? That I've been framed for this."

She smiled and clasped her hands in a single clap. "Exactly. And I know who did and how it was done."

Still frowning, nodding, he said, eagerly, "Do tell."

"They've found a gas respirator, you know, the police have. With a service number that will likely lead to you, Gordon. I don't see your mask anywhere here in your room, or on your person."

"No. It was stolen several days ago."

"I knew it!" She leaned forward conspiratorially. "These clues were planted, Gordon. And who was responsible?"

"Who?"

"I'll tell you, though it pains me, it grieves me to my core." She sighed heavily, lowered her head. "My 'friend,' your 'benefactor' . . . Stephen Glanville. Who better, with his Air Ministry connections, to help himself to your personal items, to enter inconspicuously and plant these obvious clues?"

"Why Glanville?"

"He is a notorious ladies' man, our Stephen. Though he denied knowing her, Stephen undoubtedly had an affair with Nita Ward. And he may . . . I hate to tell you this, as it may cause you pain, Gordon . . . he may have set his sights on your lovely wife."

The cadet's eyes flared. "Janet!"

"I'm afraid so. He has loitered around rehearsals, and his eyes have fallen upon her. . . . I don't believe she has given him any cause for the unforgivable thoughts he's clearly having regarding her, so I do beg you not to blame or reprove her. But with you out of the way. . . ."

"He would have a clear field," Cummins said, squinting in anger.

"Seeing your lovely wife," Agatha said, "told me everything I needed to know about you, Gordon. With such a lovely, desirable creature in your life, you would have no need for the soiled flowers of the West End."

"I love her. Janet is wonderful. I would never hurt her."

She gripped his hand again. "Then you must cling to your innocence. And I will help you, Gordon. I will plead your case. Together, we will shatter this frightful frame, and restore your good name."

He looked at her almost lovingly. "You're wonderful, Mrs. Mallowan. You're like . . . something from one of your own books."

"As are you, Gordon. As are you."

The door burst open and Inspector Greeno stood there with revolver in hand—such weapons were

checked out only when an officer felt a vital need, and
Greeno clearly felt it. His eyes widened at the sight of
Agatha, then turned hard, as he leveled the weapon at
the cadet, and behind him were two more plainclothes
detectives, equally well armed.

"Stand up, Cummins," the inspector said, "and put
your hands on your head. . . . You're nicked!"

The cadet's eyes flew to Agatha's. "Tell him, Mrs.
Mallowan! Tell them I'm innocent."

"I'll give the inspector all the details," she said gently. "Rest assured. Go quietly, dear, and it will speak
well for you."

The inspector and another detective squeezed into
the room, and the assistant handcuffed the cadet as
Greeno said more formally, "You're under arrest for
committing grievous bodily harm to Greta Heywood. . . . Take him away."

The two plainclothes men did, Cummins calling to
Agatha, "Be sure to tell him! Be sure!"

"I will," she reassured him smilingly, "I will."

When they were alone in the cubbyhole billet, the inspector asked, "What in hell are you doing here, and
what in hell was that *about*, Agatha?"

Ignoring his first question, she answered the second.
"Oh, I convinced him I believed in his innocence." She
showed the inspector the murder souvenirs on the bureau top. "I told him I believed that Stephen Glanville
had framed him for these murders, planting these clues
and others, like the respirator. . . . I assume the number
on the mask led you here?"

"It did. That's why we've arrested him only for assaulting that prostitute, Greta Heywood. We'll get 'round to willful murder charges soon enough. Why Glanville?"

"Poor Stephen and his womanizing. . . . He was a believeable suspect. With his position at the Air Ministry, he might well have framed the boy."

"That's a load of rubbish!"

"Of course it is," Agatha said pleasantly.

"Well, Cummins certainly knew Glanville didn't do it! Why would telling him that story hold any weight?"

"What was important was that it seemed a credible defense to him . . . and his counselor may eventually try to utilize it. I needed him to believe I thought him innocent, and that I would defend him to the death. . . . You may not be aware of it, Ted, but that madman saved my life, earlier, at the theater cave-in."

The inspector nodded, sighing, "I did indeed hear that. He must have thought you owed him a debt."

"I owe him no debt—he was considering killing me, as his last grand gesture. But I talked him out of it."

"My Lord, how did you manage it?"

"Oh, really, Inspector—it was easy. The boy likes my work." She gestured to the stacks of books. "He's a fan. . . . May I show you something?"

She escorted the amazed inspector into the kitchen. "With his bedroom isolated as it is, and the fire escape leading off as it does, the testimony of any of his flatmates who might say they saw him go off to bed is irrelevant."

"It is indeed," the inspector said, taking in the fire escape view. "If we can just get past those damned billet books."

She laughed, genuinely amused. "Oh, Inspector, that was my first real suspicion of our cadet. I was the wife of an RAF pilot, in the first war—I know all about billet books and men covering up for each other, as they sneak in and out to see their sweethearts and wives . . . not necessarily in that order."

"Blimey, I never thought it—it's bleedin' obvious, if you'll pardon me saying."

"It's a trick immemorial, in service camps, Inspector. Oh, they'll fuss and moan, when you try to prove it— tell you you'll blow the billet wide open, if you expose the practice. But take my word: that so-called passbook is a tissue of lies. . . . Do you have a pen, Inspector?"

"I believe so," he said, and dug it out. Then, a grin splitting the bulldog face, he added, *"Two* pens, counting the one Cummins copped from the Jouannet flat."

She sat at the little kitchen table—which was cluttered with the dishes of RAF cadets—and cleared a place. She signed the title page of *Evil Under the Sun* and then inscribed on the flyleaf: "To Gordon Cummins—a reader I will never forget. A.C., St. John's Wood, 1942."

With a smile, she handed the book to the flabbergasted inspector, saying, "See to it Mr. Cummins gets it, will you?"

AFTER . . .

Detective Chief Inspector Edward Greeno, Sir Bernard Spilsbury and Frederick Cherrill mounted an airtight case against Airman Gordon Frederick Cummins.

The items Agatha had found in the cadet's billet were identified as belongings of murder victims Doris Jouannet and Nita Ward. The fingerprints on the candlestick and the tumbler of beer from the Lowe flat were Cummins's. Greta Heywood and Phyllis O'Dwyer identified Cummins as their would-be assailant (they shared the tabloid reward money).

Sir Bernard Spilsbury matched sand, grit and cement dust from the gas mask's fabric to samples from the air-raid shelter where Evelyn Hamilton's body had been found. Items belonging to Miss Hamilton were also found in the billet, and the two five-pound notes Phyllis

O'Dwyer had turned in to Inspector Greeno were traced to Cummins, through RAF pay records.

As Agatha had predicted, the billet passbooks had been falsified, cadets covering up for cadets out-on-the-town. But other RAF airmen were just as eager *not* to cover up for Cummins, whom they did not particularly like: the nicknames of the "Duke" and the "Count," which Cummins claimed as his, had been seized upon derisively by fellow cadets offended by Cummins's constant boasting about his "noble" birth. They said he often got dressed up in his best civilian clothes, affecting an upper-class accent, going out to impress prostitutes.

"And him with such a beauty for a missus," one cadet had said, shaking his head.

Other cadets confirmed that they'd seen Cummins throwing money around, in his "Count" persona, shortly after Evelyn Hamilton's murder. The Hamilton woman, of course, had been stripped not only of her life but of eighty pounds.

Throughout, Cummins maintained his innocence as well as a sunny, confident disposition. His wife, Janet, remained loyal and claimed to believe his story of having been framed by a "higher-up" at the Air Ministry. Janet even managed to mount a petition seeking a stay of execution until the "mystery man" who "switched gas masks" with poor Gordon could be found.

Despite this effort, shortly before eight a.m. on June 25, 1942, Gordon Cummins strolled, a smiling self-proclaimed innocent martyr, to the gallows. His wife wept; working girls, eager to return to the dimly lit streets behind Piccadilly in relative safety, cheered. The clatter of the falling trapdoor punctuated the distant thunder of explosions.

Luftwaffe planes were flying over London, on a rare daylight bombing raid.

Agatha's new play received glowing reviews. It moved to the Cambridge Theatre for a long run, and opened in New York in June, 1944, under the sanitized title *Ten Little Indians*, where it ran for an impressive 426 performances.

The great tragedy of the war for Agatha was the death of her daughter's husband; but Rosalind and Hubert's son, Matthew, would be the love of Mrs. Mallowan's later life.

Toward the end of the war, after a weekend visit in Wales with Rosalind and grandchild Matthew, Agatha returned to Lawn Road Flats. Exhausted and chilled to the bone, she switched on the heat and began to cook up some kippers, when Max came home, unexpectedly early, from his service in North Africa.

It was as if he'd only left yesterday—though he, too, was two-stone heavier. He had eaten well, overseas, while potatoes and bread had taken their toll on Agatha, who was frankly relieved her husband had added girth, as well. The kippers had burned during the excitement of the homecoming, but they sat together and ate the oily things in glee and had the most wonderfully mundane evening of their married lives.

She never told Max about the Ripper affair, and their friend Stephen Glanville discreetly never mentioned it, either.

Sir Bernard, who was himself struggling with an on-again-off-again autobiography, said to her toward the end of the affair, "This will make an interesting tidbit for your autobiography."

"I believe I'll leave this bit out," she told him, and she did.

She felt foolish about how she'd endangered herself, going to Cummins's flat, and preferred Max not know of it; and she had resolved any misgivings she'd had about the inappropriateness of her fiction in the post-war world. Good and evil were a reality, and fiction that dealt with that subject, however escapist in intent, would always have a place.

One good thing had come of the episode, however: she never again had the Gunman dream.

Perhaps, at long last, her subconscious had banished the nightmare, out of her acceptance of one of the primary themes of her own work: that behind innocent eyes, evil often lurked. The thought wasn't a frightening one, once you'd adapted it to your thinking.

At least not so frightening as to cause nightmares.

At the incessant urging of Stephen Glanville, Agatha indeed wrote an ancient-Egyptian mystery, *Death Comes at the End*, published in 1945; also, she dedicated the next Poirot, *Five Little Pigs* (1943), to her persistent friend. Glanville, after a distinguished career concluding with his position as Herbert Thompson Professor of Egyptology at Cambridge, died at age fifty-six, the premature death greatly grieving the Mallowans.

Agatha modeled the country home setting of *The Hollow* (1946) after that of actor Larry Sullivan and his wife Danae's estate at Haselmere, Surrey, dedicating the novel to them with apologies.

With her husband home and the war winding down, Agatha left her position in the dispensary at University College Hospital. She and Sir Bernard Spilsbury remained friendly, but drifted apart.

In November 1945, she was sad to learn that another tragedy had befallen Sir Bernard, who had never really gotten over the death of his son, Peter: another son, Alan, had fallen ill with galloping consumption, and soon died. She and Max attended the funeral, and later had a pleasant lunch with Bernard, but despite a superficial air of normality, the great man had clearly failed.

Spilsbury soon suffered several minor strokes, but Agatha understood he was continuing to work with his usual dedication, testifying in trials, conducting postmortems, endlessly filling little file cards with data and theories. On December 17, 1947, as fastidiously dressed as ever, Sir Bernard Spilsbury turned on the gas in the little laboratory down the hall from the dispensary where Agatha had worked.

Inspector Greeno suffered no such melancholy. After thirty-eight years on the job, he retired from Scotland Yard in 1960. As head of the Yard's number one district—covering the West End and Soho—he'd long been the "Guv'ner" to coppers and crooks alike.

The *Daily Express* said of Greeno's retirement, "His record of successful murder investigation, including the notorious Blackout Ripper case, bears comparison with any police force in the world. One thing is certain: the underworld will be celebrating tonight."

Agatha Christie Mallowan lived a long and happy and productive later life, with Max Mallowan at her side. Her play *The Mousetrap* outdid *Ten Little Indians* and became a West End institution.

Shortly before her death in 1976, Agatha allowed the publication of the Poirot novel she'd written during the Blitz, to best-selling results, the death of the Belgian sleuth rating a front-page obituary in the *New York Times*. Her Miss Marple novel, salted away at the same time, published shortly after the author's passing, was similarly a best-seller.

While Agatha Christie is immortal, Gordon Cummins and his crimes have, like Mrs. Mallowan's Gunman, gone the way of all nightmares—an unpleasantness forgotten upon waking.

Applause in the Dark

Author's Note: the reader is advised not to peruse this bibliographic essay prior to finishing the novel.

The previous novels in what has been called by others my "disaster" series have featured real-life crime-fiction writers as detectives in fact-based mysteries, often in settings and situations where they had actually been—i.e., Jacques Futrelle on the *Titanic* and Edgar Rice Burroughs at Pearl Harbor during the attack. Agatha Christie, of course, did live through the London Blitz. The description of her daily life—her work in a hospital dispensary, her writing projects and habits, etc.—has a strictly factual basis.

Agatha Christie was adept at sleight of hand, and the trick this book attempts is to present a true-crime story in the guise of a traditional mystery. How well I've succeeded is up to the reader, but the challenge of it was the sort of writing problem Mrs. Mallowan might well have relished.

That the real-life murders in question were vicious sex crimes of course contrasts with the cozy image of Agatha Christie (not entirely deserved in my view); but, among other things attempted in these pages, it was my wish to reflect upon reality versus fantasy, and the role of mystery and crime fiction in a brutal world. At the same time, I hoped not to dishonor Agatha's memory by handling the subject matter in a manner she might have found in poor taste.

The series of murders by the so-called Blackout Ripper did occur, in the time frame indicated, and the basic facts of the case are honored here, as much as conflicting source material and the passage of time allow. I chose to keep the crimes of Gordon Cummins in their proper time frame, and—despite the title of this book—not at the height of the Blitz in 1940. This is, however, a work of fiction, and liberties have been taken, including the shifting of certain events to form a better-flowing narrative.

While my involvement of Agatha Christie in the Blackout Ripper murder investigation is fanciful, the creator of Hercule Poirot and Jane Marple did indeed work side by side with the famous pathologist, Sir Bernard Spilsbury, at University College Hospital during this period. The discovery that these two giants of the world of crime—a celebrated writer of mystery fiction and the British father of forensics—knew each other within an intimate work environment, at a time when both of these lonely older people were separated from their spouses, gave impetus to this narrative.

I intend this novel as a valentine to Agatha Christie, whose work—and life—I much admire. As a writer who has been identified throughout my career with the hard-boiled school of crime fiction, this choice of protagonist may seem bizarre to some of my regular readers. Suffice to say I do not view Christie as a "cozy" writer, but a tough-minded storyteller whose worldview is harder-edged than most *noir* authors, and whose primary detectives—Poirot and Miss Marple— are, beneath their deceiving surfaces, as relentless and even vengeful as Mike Hammer or my own Nate Heller.

Christie has in common with two hard-boiled writers I much admire—Mickey Spillane and Erle Stanley Gardner—huge success and scant respect. These enormously popular and influential writers are dismissed as simplistic storytellers, with even their admirers often praising them in a left-handed, patronizing fashion. I hope, in these pages, that I have given some small sense of the serious, gifted writer this woman was.

Many have considered Christie an enigmatic figure, and it is my hope that the character study in these pages has done her justice and in some measure brought her alive.

Books on Christie's life and work are often inconsistent where dates are concerned; even Agatha and her husband Max Mallowan are themselves inconsistent, in their respective autobiographies, about when exactly Max left London to serve in North Africa. Even so, I

have taken certain liberties here that go beyond the in-
consistencies of my sources.

The prime example of this artistic license is my moving up in time the writing and production of the unfortunately named *Ten Little Niggers*, so that it would
coincide with the Blackout Ripper murders; the material
here relating to the problems that Agatha had with that
tasteless title, and the title changes that ensued, is accurate. The St. James Theatre did suffer bomb damage (in
1943) and the production was indeed forced to move.

Most of the characters in this novel are real people,
and the others are fictional characters with real-life counterparts. All of these characterizations, however fact-
based they may be, must be viewed as fictionalized; and
the characterizations range from those of Agatha, Sir
Bernard Spilsbury and Edward Greeno—about whom
book-length works have been written—to minor players
who appear only in passing in reference material.

Gordon Cummins's wife was indeed a secretary to a
theatrical producer; I have given her the name "Janet,"
and she must be viewed as a largely fictional character.
Producer and director Bertram Morris and Irene Helier
are fictional, with real-life counterparts. My portrayals
of Francis L. Sullivan (who did portray Poirot on stage,
twice) and Stephen Glanville (a distinguished colleague
of Max Mallowan's) draw largely on Agatha's own autobiography and the official Christie biography by Janet
Morgan.

The victims of the Blackout Ripper appear here under
their real names. According to several sources, Margaret

Lowe's teenaged daughter did prompt the discovery of her mother's body; however, the name "Mary Jane" is invented, though the backstory has a factual basis. The two women who escaped the Ripper's clutches are given their real names.

My longtime research associate, George Hagenauer, spent many hours digging out material and working with me to explore the possibilities of interweaving Agatha Christie's Blitz-era experiences with the Blackout Ripper case. While I myself uncovered the Cummins case in seeking an appropriate crime for Agatha's involvement, it was George who discovered the Christie/Spilsbury connection, which proved so crucial to this effort. Among the material George turned up was the article "London Strangler" by Clyde Black, *Detective World*, July 1952, perhaps the single best treatment of the case, despite the obscurity of the source.

Agatha Christie's *An Autobiography* (1977) is a massive, detailed but wonderful work, and much more revealing about its author than many would have it. The autobiographical works *Come Tell Me How You Live* (1946), bylined Agatha Christie Mallowan, and *Mallowan's Memoirs* (1977), by Max Mallowan, were also consulted. Particularly useful was the aforementioned, first-rate authorized biography, *Agatha Christie* (1984) by Janet Morgan.

I am partial to two books that discuss both Christie's life and her works: *Agatha Christie: The Woman and her Mysteries* (1990) by Gillian Gill; and *The Life and Crimes of Agatha Christie* (2001) by Charles Osborne, who has adapted several of Christie's plays into novel form.

Surprisingly, one of the best Christie overviews is disguised as a picture book: *The World of Agatha Christie* (1999) by Martin Fido (whose Blackout Ripper article, coincidentally—mentioned below—first attracted me to the Cummins case). Another work vital to this novel was *The Getaway Guide to Agatha Christie's England* (1999) by Judith Hurdle.

Many of Christie's works were referred to, notably her *The Mousetrap and Other Plays* (1978), which includes *Ten Little Indians*. Various other books on Christie were delved into: *Agatha Christie A to Z* (1996), Dawn B. Sova, Ph.D.; *Agatha Christie: First Lady of Crime* (1977), edited by H.R.F. Keating; *Murder She Wrote: A Study of Agatha Christie's Detective Fiction* (1982), Patricia D. Maida and Nicholas B. Spornick; *The Mysterious World of Agatha Christie* (1975), Jeffrey Feinman; and *The New Bedside, Bathtub and Armchair Companion to Agatha Christie* (1992), edited by Dick Riley and Pam McAllister. Robert Barnard's *A Talent to Deceive: An Appreciation of Agatha Christie* (1979, 1980), while interesting, is typical of the supposedly pro-Christie critics who underestimate her abilities.

Book-length works on the principal detectives in the case proved particularly fruitful: *The Scalpel of Scotland Yard: The Life of Sir Bernard Spilsbury* (1952), Douglas G. Browne and E. V. Tullett; *War on the Underworld* (1960), Ex-Detective Chief Superintendent Edward Greeno, M.B.E. (who appears to be the inspiration for John Thaw's "Regan" character on the popular 1970s UK television series, *The Sweeney*); and *Cherrill of the Yard* (1954), Fred Cherrill. All of these have chapters devoted to the Blackout Ripper. The most detailed, ironically, is in the autobiography of Cherrill, the fingerprint expert whose presence in this novel is largely peripheral.

This novel is the first book-length work on the Blackout Ripper murder spree, which is largely unknown in the United States, allowing me the conceit of presenting a true-crime case in mystery format. Hardcore true-crime buffs in the UK may recognize this case, as it has been frequently written up in British true-crime anthologies and overviews.

Among the UK publications of that type that were consulted are *The Chronicle of Crime* (1993), Martin Fido; Volumes Eight and Seventeen of *Crimes and Punishment: A Pictorial Encyclopedia of Aberrant Behavior* (1974), edited by Jackson Morley; and *The Detectives: Crime and Detection in Fact and Fiction* (1978), Frank Smyth and Myles Ludwig. A British weekly publication, *Murder Casebook: Investigations in the Ultimate Crime*, Issue 72 (1991), "Blackout Killers," was particularly helpful (another George Hagenauer find).

Where the Blitz era in London is concerned, I leaned heavily on one book—*London at War* (1995) by Phillip Ziegler—and I offer my sincere thanks to the author. Other helpful books on the Blitz era include *The Homefront: The British and the Second World War* (1976), Arthur Marwick; *Keep Smiling Through: The Home*

Front 1939–45 (1975), Susan Briggs; *The London Blitz* (1980), David Johnson; and the delightful picture book *The Wartime Scrapbook: From Blitz to Victory 1939–1945* (1995), compiled by Robert Opie.

I make no pretense at being knowledgeable about London and any errors herein, geographical and otherwise, are my own. To whatever degree I have been accurate, however, I owe thanks to a "walking guide" book, providing key information about Blitz-vintage London: *The Face of London* by Harold P. Clunn, an undated volume circa 1956; this was yet another George Hagenauer discovery. A helpful volume on crime and policework was *London After Dark* (1954) by Ex-Superintendent Robert Fabian.

I am extremely grateful to my editor, Natalee Rosenstein of Berkley Prime Crime, for her patience. An ambitious but misjudged false start on this novel—patterned upon Christie's *The Murder of Roger Ackroyd* (narrated by Cummins!)—required a request for a deadline extension, which Natalee kindly granted.

This enabled my wife, writer Barbara Collins, and me to take advantage of a trip to London for the premiere of the film *Road to Perdition* and visit numerous of the actual locations, from Agatha's Lawn Road flat to every murder site. Thank you to driver Rudi Allman of Hanover Chauffeurs, whose driving was far superior to Sir Bernard Spilsbury's.

Thanks also to my friend and agent Dominick Abel, who lent his usual support during a busy, trying time. My wife helped out by reading Agatha's wonderful but long autobiography so that we could discuss and explore Agatha's character, in my attempt to solve the mystery of Christie. For many months we listened to unabridged audios of Poirot novels ordered from the UK, and read by actors David Suchet and Hugh Fraser; never has research been such a pleasure.

About the Author

MAX ALLAN COLLINS has earned an unprecedented twelve Private Eye Writers of America "Shamus" nominations for his historical thrillers, winning twice for his Nathan Heller novels, *True Detective* (1983) and *Stolen Away* (1991). In 2002 he was presented the "Herodotus" Lifetime Achievement Award by the Historical Mystery Appreciation Society.

A Mystery Writers of America "Edgar" nominee in both fiction and non-fiction categories, Collins has been hailed as "the Renaissance man of mystery fiction." His credits include five suspense novel series, film criticism, short fiction, songwriting, trading-card sets, and movie/TV tie-in novels, including *In the Line of Fire*, *Air Force One*, and the *New York Times* bestselling *Saving Private Ryan*. His many books on popular culture include the award-winning *Elvgren: His Life and Art* and *The History of Mystery*, which was nominated for every major mystery award.

His graphic novel *Road to Perdition* is the basis of the Academy Award-winning DreamWorks feature film starring Tom Hanks, Paul Newman and Jude Law, directed by Sam Mendes. He scripted the internationally syndicated comic strip "Dick Tracy" from 1977 to 1993, is co-creator of the comic-book features "Ms. Tree," "Wild Dog," and "Mike Danger," has written the "Batman" comic book and newspaper strip, and several comics mini-series, including "Johnny Dynamite" and "CSI: Crime Scene Investigation," based on the hit TV series for which he has also written a bestselling series of novels and two video games.

As an independent filmmaker in his native Iowa, he wrote and directed the suspense film "Mommy," starring Patty McCormack, premiering on Lifetime in 1996, and a 1997 sequel, "Mommy's Day." The recipient of a record eight Iowa Motion Picture Awards for screenplays, he wrote "The Expert," a 1995 HBO World Premiere; and wrote and directed the award-winning documentary "Mike Hammer's Mickey Spillane" (1999) and the innovative "Real Time: Siege at Lucas Street Market" (2000).

Collins lives in Muscatine, Iowa, with his wife, writer Barbara Collins; their son Nathan is a computer science major at the University of Iowa.